THE YOUNGEST SUSPECT

Karan Khanna

PEGGY MOHAN was born in Trinidad, West Indies. She has taught linguistics, made television programmes for children, been a cartoon animator and has twice been an expert witness responsible for analyzing confessional statements in terrorism trials. She now teaches music at the Vasant Valley School, New Delhi, and is also the author of another book, *Jahajin*, also published by HarperCollins India.

ALSO BY PEGGY MOHAN

Jahajin, HarperCollins Publishers India, 2007

Praise for *Jahajin*

'In *Jahajin*, Mohan has produced an example of [auto-ethnography] with the compelling ring of truth.' —*Outlook*

'. . . and we understand the many shades of migration that can occur in a single journey – through which the Chinidads ultimately become Trinidads for the migrant.' —*Deccan Herald*

'Unadorned but evocative, *Jahajin* comprehends complicated, problematic literary issues [. . .] through the smallest particle: experience.' —*First City*

'Peggy has seamlessly entwined metaphors in the tale, pulling, as she says, one level of story to the other.' —*The Hindu*

THE YOUNGEST SUSPECT

Peggy Mohan

HarperCollins *Publishers* India
a joint venture with

New Delhi

First published in India in 2012 by
HarperCollins *Publishers* India
a joint venture with
The India Today Group

Copyright © Peggy Mohan 2012

ISBN: 978-93-5029-383-6

2 4 6 8 10 9 7 5 3 1

Peggy Mohan asserts the moral right to be identified as
the author of this work.

HarperCollins *Publishers*
A-53, Sector 57, Noida 201301, India
77-85 Fulham Palace Road, London W6 8JB, United Kingdom
Hazelton Lanes, 55 Avenue Road, Suite 2900, Toronto, Ontario M5R 3L2
and 1995 Markham Road, Scarborough, Ontario M1B 5M8, Canada
25 Ryde Road, Pymble, Sydney, NSW 2073, Australia
31 View Road, Glenfield, Auckland 10, New Zealand
10 East 53rd Street, New York NY 10022, USA

Typeset in 11/14 Requiem Regular at
SÜRYA

Printed and bound at
Thomson Press (India) Ltd.

for Adil,
wherever he may be.

We both are lost, and alone in the world,
Walk with me, in the gentle rain,
Don't be afraid, I've a hand for your hand,
And I will be your life, for a while . . .

—Luiz Bonfá/Matt Dubey,
The Gentle Rain

1

The Sabarmati Express to Ahmedabad was running late. At least five hours late, Adil thought. He dozed restlessly as he waited on the platform at Meghnagar, fretting about his Twelfth Board Exams, less than three weeks away. The train pulled into the station just before sunrise.

He found his coach, S6. It was bursting with people. He had never seen a rail bogie so full. Besides the usual families and quiet men travelling alone, there were a number of loud young men who seemed to be travelling ticketless, all part of the same group. Kar sevaks, they called themselves. They were on their way back from Ayodhya, where others like them had demolished the Babri Masjid ten years ago.

He lowered his gaze to avoid eye contact with them, and tried to find his seat.

An old woman frowned at him as he approached, and pointed vaguely at the floor. The seats, she said, were not for children, they were for adults. He was young. He would have to 'adjust'.

He found himself a spot in the aisle and shrank into it.

He had barely managed to fall asleep again when the train

pulled into a station and half the passengers rushed out of the carriage to get their morning chai. Daylight. *'Jai Shri Ram, Jai Shri Ram.'* Adil could hear the kar sevaks raising slogans all along the platform.

Then suddenly they rushed back inside and started closing the shutters on the windows. The train started again.

Suddenly they heard the loud sound of a bombardment from the platform side. The carriage was being pelted with the sharp fist-sized stones that lay between the wooden sleepers on the track.

Someone pulled the chain and the train stopped.

Adil sat up. The doors opened again and more kar sevaks rushed into the coach. They instantly locked the doors behind them and began barricading them with luggage to keep out the crowd of stone-pelters, and then rushed to close the shutters on all the remaining windows on the platform side.

The train started again.

Suddenly Adil's nostrils twitched. Smoke. Thick, black, poisonous. Coiling up in a cloud towards the ceiling. And already burning hot.

He recognized the smell: it was the smell of burning foam. Adil remembered reading somewhere that foam inside the seats would release hydrogen cyanide when it burnt.

Hydrogen cyanide! Gas chamber smoke! He turned his head sharply, looking for the source.

A lower berth near the door, just two compartments away. Smouldering.

He leapt to his feet and headed for the opposite door.

The smoke and heat increased as they struggled to shift all

the luggage blocking the exit. The crowd pressed forward, but the door stayed firmly shut. The heat was now glowing down at them from the ceiling. Adil felt his ears begin to burn.

He bent his head away from the radiant heat and saw a woman far behind him in the queue faint. He held his breath.

For a split second the pressure shifted, and he felt himself being flung backward. The door was yanked open and the crowd lurched forward again. Now he was sailing, out, out, out the open door, out into the vestibule towards the other door, on the Signal Falia side.

He paused for a heartbeat at the ladder to marvel at how far down the ground really was.

And then . . . he jumped.

2

I let my class go five minutes early, grabbed my strolley bag and hurried down to the bus stop. Ramya's taxi was already there. I slid in the back seat beside her and we headed for the airport.

'The flight is delayed. An hour,' she said, undoing the hooks of the stiff legal collar she wore over her sari blouse in court. Her sari was shot silk, and silvery grey. 'Feel like stopping for coffee?'

'Sure,' I nodded. 'You can brief me about the case.'

We pulled in to Cafe Coffee Day and took a table in the corner.

'Ok, Deepi. What do you want to know?'

'The background. Why those fourteen boys were arrested. And I'd like to know if they are guilty.'

'They aren't. They were picked up and charged with planting bombs around Ahmedabad.'

Trust Ramya to get me into something like this.

'Small bombs,' she clarified helpfully. 'And most of them didn't go off.'

Bombs. I put the thought on hold. 'And you think the boys are being framed.'

'Yes.' She paused. 'Remember the politician who was shot the year after the riots? In Ahmedabad?'

'Of course.'

'Well the Gujarat government was feeling some heat. People were saying that the government had him bumped off. So they went and arrested the boys as a distraction.'

'A distraction?'

'The bomb incident happened almost a year before the politician was killed. And the case had been closed. No leads. To be reopened only if there was fresh discovery. Then the police applied to reopen it right after the politician's death, and suddenly found all these boys.'

'I see.' I paused. 'I remember that killing. A politician found dead in his car near Law Garden. Five bullets in him, but strangely not much blood.' I paused: how to say this? 'And one shot fired . . . from below.'

'Through the left testicle. The bullet went all the way up to his shoulder.'

'Yes. Without even spilling any blood. A "fuck-you" shot.'

'What!' Ramya's eyebrows shot up.

'I remember reading about an identical killing somewhere. Well, it was almost identical . . .'

Ramya frowned. 'Must be one of your whodunits.'

'Murder mystery. It starts with a body in a cable car, same low angle shot from a gun pressed against the man's anus. The detective guesses fast that *that* shot was not the cause of death, it must have been done after the other shots. In fact, probably after the man was dead. Point is, it's a vindictive shot. Unnecessary, and full of hate. It just reeks of an execution. What cops would do to someone about to rat on them.' I shook my head. 'The guy who did it was obviously a pro.'

'Hmm . . .' She nodded, sipped her coffee. Changed gears back to the present. 'This is a POTA case.'

It would have to be, or she wouldn't have called me. POTA, the draconian Prevention of Terrorism Act, passed by Parliament the same year as the Godhra train fire. Under POTA, a confession made to the police would be treated as an admission of guilt. The suspect would not have the right to deny the confession later in court.

'And this whole case hinges on the confessions,' I guessed.

'Right. Unlike the Afzal case, this is the only thing they have against the boys.' She looked up at me. 'By the way, the Appeal Court threw out the confession in the Afzal case too. It overturned the verdict of the POTA court.'

'They didn't release him.'

'But they threw out the confession. I just want you to manage that for us again.' She stood up. 'Let's go.'

Our taxi stopped in a line of traffic at the Mahipalpur red light. Another line of traffic bound for the airport piled up on our right, hemming us in.

'Oh, just to warn you,' Ramya's voice came again, softly. 'These confessions are not in English. They're in Gujarati.'

'You're *kidding*!' I turned to stare at her.

She shook her head. 'But there's a whole team there to help you. I even have two court scribes on the job . . .'

'Ramya . . .' I sputtered, 'you're mad. The prosecution will *slay* me. I don't know Gujarati!'

'It's the same quantitative analysis you have to do,' she soothed me. 'No need to get worried.'

'But . . . but . . . why are we doing this? Why are *we* going all the way from Delhi for this case? There are enough lawyers in Ahmedabad.'

'No, there aren't. Not senior lawyers. They have all been threatened. Not one of them is willing to take the case.'

Gujarati, I thought. I had been to Ahmedabad many times, but had never got a fix on the language, had never needed to learn it. The rickshawalas and shopkeepers would make out at once that I was from the north and speak to me in Hindi. And all my friends' kids who had gone to NID, the National Institute of Design in Ahmedabad, seemed to come back to Delhi without having picked up any Gujarati either.

No, I shook my head. I can manage. I *can* follow Gujarati, if I don't have to talk. Follow maybe . . . 65 per cent. No, 70 per cent. That's enough. And these confessions wouldn't be colloquial stuff anyway: straight legal language is always easier. Lots of key nouns in common with Hindi. I could pick up on the function words, some phrases. And I can take my time, ask questions. It's always easier following people who don't know English: it's the English speakers who use their other language to hide.

'You have all night to soak it up,' Ramya cut in smoothly. 'And the morning too. The hearing isn't till tomorrow afternoon.'

'Thanks!' I snapped.

We checked in for the flight and went through security. Sat down to wait again. There was another time I had had to sit and listen to a personal narrative and pretend that I understood it all. In Ranchi, an old woman was talking to me in Sadri, telling me about something that happened long ago. From time to time, she would stop and cock her head at me, waiting for a sign that I was following what she was saying. And I would nod. I didn't want her to switch to Hindi to make it easier for me. I had needed samples of Sadri speech.

'Ramya . . .'

She turned and looked at me.

'Remember last time? When we wanted to show the court what a real confession statement should look like? I asked the court recorder to show the messy thing he had typed up as my testimony. Full of x-ed out text? Not at all like the clean-and-neat police confession. Well I have an idea. If you can set it up.'

'What?'

'I want to videotape some mock confessions. In Gujarati. With similar boys and your professional scribes, in the same frame. I need you to arrange a video camera and a cameraman. And a few Muslim boys. I want to show what a scribe goes through when he has to keep up with the speed of normal speech.' I paused as a thought struck me. 'They wouldn't be typed, would they? These confessions. They wouldn't have had typed them in Gujarati. Wouldn't have had a fast program back then.'

'No, they're hand-written.'

'Great! We get to look at handwriting! I want to show how our scribe tries to slow down the speaker, to be able to keep up. What he writes as against what we get on the tape. Then we can compare our confessions with the police ones.' I was warming to the idea more and more. 'We'll submit the videotapes to the court too. The tapes will have an unbroken time code, proof that they are unedited recordings.' I grinned. 'A nice techie touch. The judge will love it.'

Ramya whipped out her cell phone and spoke urgently for a moment.

'Done,' she said, clicking off.

'Now I really have to learn this language in a flash!'

The seats around us began to fill up. Outside, the sky was getting dark.

'You'll do the interviews?' Ramya asked suddenly.

'No, it won't be like that, question and answer,' I replied. 'That's no use to us. Too much stop-and-start. Not like a confession at all. If I'm to compare the time *we* take with the time recorded in the police log, I'll need continuous speech. A flow I can time in words per minute.'

'How will you get them to talk like that?'

'See,' I said, 'I don't give a rat's ass *what* they say. I just want the boys to keep talking. So that the scribes can keep writing. But I don't want them to know we're only interested in *how* they're speaking. That would screw up the data.'

A story, I thought. I need them to concentrate on telling me a story. Something amazing that happened in the past.

A day they would never forget . . .

'I know! I'll ask them to talk about what happened the day after Godhra.'

A squawk over the loudspeaker told us it was time to board. We found our seats and buckled up.

'What about the judge?' I asked. 'Another Dhingra?'

'No,' Ramya shook her head. 'This time the judge is a woman.'

'Wow!' I beamed. 'A woman – that's great!'

'No, it isn't,' Ramya growled. 'She's tough as nails. And she comes from a conservative Hindu family. I only hope she isn't going to be hostile.'

I sat back, deflated. Here we go again.

'Don't get too antsy, though. Just take it as it comes.'

'Yeah.' I looked out the window. The plane in front of us was already racing down the runway. We edged forward to go next. 'Well, you never know.'

The bass notes began to rumble and our engines revved up for takeoff. Like a cat, tail twitching, butt in the air, the plane gathered up the energy to spring. I felt the familiar buzz of an adventure about to start and sank back into my seat, ready to fly.

'Oh, I forgot to ask you,' Ramya's voice faded on as soon as we were airborne. 'What do we say is your fee this time?'

I groaned. 'The old Catch-22 question . . . If I want money for this, they'll say I'm just a mercenary, that I'll say anything to get the client off. And if I don't, then I'm a terrorist myself. Great!'

She laughed. 'But seriously. What? So that you and I at least know you're not a terrorist.'

I was about to put her off again, but then her sari gleamed at me. Aha! '*That's* what I want,' I decided then and there. 'That sari you're wearing.'

'*This?*' She looked down incredulously. 'But it isn't even new!'

'It'll do.'

'*Take* it!' she exclaimed. 'But I need it tomorrow.'

'I don't want it now. Only when we win the case.'

She rolled her eyes. 'Then you'll have to wait a long time. It'll be a rag by then. You know how these things go.'

'Fine with me. But this fee is going to sound unbelievable in court.' I grinned.

The captain switched off the seatbelt sign and the stewardess came round with tetra packs of juice. Ramya waved her away.

'We'll probably be up all night,' she yawned, closing her eyes. 'I'm going to get some sleep. You should too.'

When we reached Ahmedabad, it was already dark. The plane came to a halt and we went down the steps onto the tarmac. A short walk and we were inside the terminal.

Ramya strode through the building like an empress and out the front door. A little past the porch, a car was waiting for us. A young man opened the door for us and we got in the back. Then he got in next to the driver and we were off.

I stared at the billboards in Gujarati as we drove into the city. The Gujarati script resembled Devanagari a bit, though it didn't have a line on top. I couldn't actually read it, but it did remind me a little of an old writing system that I had seen as a child. Kaithi. That was the script that court scribes in north India had used for everything till about a hundred years ago. My grandfather had had old books in Kaithi. He had even tried to teach me once how to write it.

And then I remembered that this case was going to be about the work of scribes. And that I was a Kayasth too. I came from a family whose men had once worked as scribes in the Mughal courts. Scribes who had taken down testimony. And confessions.

Papa, I thought. I'd better call Papa tonight. And ask him what he knows about court scribes in Gujarat.

Our car stopped in the porch of a large grim-looking hotel. We got out and went up the stairs to the suite that was Ramya's headquarters. The place was humming like a newsroom. A number of bright-eyed trainees darted about from desk to desk, with copies of documents in their hands, stopping to confer urgently with this colleague or that. Ramya waved to two older men who looked up from a pile of papers, calling them over to meet me.

'This is Anoop. And this is Jaafer-bhai. Both are trained scribes. They will help you with the confession statements.'

Anoop nodded timidly. Jaafer-bhai gave me a broad smile.

'Hi,' I began. 'Can I see one? One of the confessions? Get a first impression?'

Jaafer-bhai went and looked through the stack on his desk, and stopped at one. Took it out and brought it over to me.

'This one, Madam, youngest suspect. Only eighteen years when they arrest him. Only!'

I took the Photostat copy and tried to make out the boy's name.

'Name is Adil Ansari, Madam,' Jaafer-bhai supplied. 'He is resident of Jamalpur colony, Ahmedabad. I tell you what is there?'

'In a while, Jaafer-bhai.' I smiled to soften the dismissal. 'Just let me look at the writing first.'

'You just say when you are ready, Madam,' he said, and he and Anoop returned to their desk.

I stared at the dim grey paper on my desk and emptied my mind. The handwriting was neat, unbelievably neat, and even: every line was properly aligned to an imaginary left margin. I flipped through the pages, looking for scratches, corrections. None. No abbreviations either. The scribe who had written this was not at all pressed for time.

I looked at the time-in recorded on the top of the page: 5.35 p.m.

Suddenly I felt myself transported to a room in a gloomy sepia-toned office building. A large hand came into focus, holding a tiny fountain pen. Then the image zoomed out to show a man in his mid-thirties with short hair and a moustache and the beginnings of a tummy. He was wearing a khaki uniform. It was evening. The man worked alone by the light of a desk lamp. Every few seconds, he would look up from what he was writing to consult his rough notes. And then he would start to write again, carefully.

He was making a 'fair copy'.

Then I remembered what I had wanted to ask Papa: Gujarati was clearly faster to take dictation in than Hindi, but it wasn't all that fast. I was certain that scribes in olden days would not have used this modern Gujarati script for fast note-taking. There would have been something else they used in the courts. Not Kaithi, but something similar. Something from this part of India.

I went over to the window, took out my cell phone and called Papa.

He picked up on the third ring. 'Hel-*lo*?'

'Hi, Papa. It's Deepa. I need some information.'

'Where are you, Deepa?' his voice sang across the airwaves.

'I'm in Ahmedabad, Papa. I'm working on a case. A POTA case. I'm looking at some confession statements.'

'I didn't know you were going out of Delhi!'

'I'll be back tomorrow night. Papa, the confessions are in Gujarati, and they're hand-written. I wanted to know something about court scribes in this part of India. There must be Kayasths in Gujarat.'

'Yes.'

'But they wouldn't have written in Kaithi, would they? In the old days? I sort of remember that there was a similar script that was used for Marathi and Gujarati. But I can't remember the name.'

'It was . . .' his speech began to break up.

'Papa? *Papa!* I didn't get that. Could you spell it for me?'

'M-O-D-I,' his voice was faint. 'Can you hear me better now?'

'Yes!' I exulted. 'Thanks! See you!' I clicked off.

Modi, I thought. This is going to sound fantastic.

'Madam,' Jaafer-bhai's voice, over my shoulder. 'They have come. The boys you asked for. And the camera. They are downstairs. Please come.'

Jaafer-bhai and Anoop led me back down the stairs to a conference room near the front door. A long table with chairs all around it took up most of the room. Three boys sat waiting timidly on the far side, all wearing skullcaps. A cameraman stood near the door with a Betacam video camera already up on a tripod.

I took Jaafer-bhai and Anoop aside to brief them.

'Just tell them we want them to talk about what happened in their colonies the day after Godhra. Tell them they have to speak in Gujarati.'

'In Gujarati.' He nodded.

'The reason it has to be in Gujarati is that we want to compare what they say with some confessions we have from boys who were arrested. That we don't believe the confessions are genuine. That Muslim boys would ever say the things that are in the confessions.'

'Right, Madam.'

'We'll do them one at a time. One of the boys will give his testimony, and one of you will sit next to him and write down what he is saying. In longhand. You can ask questions, but mostly I want the boys to do the talking.' I looked around a moment. 'We'll keep the camera right where it is. And I'll sit down there . . .' I pointed to a chair across the table from the boys. 'Tell them I will understand whatever they say: no need for them to speak in Hindi or Urdu.'

Jaafer-bhai nodded and took his place, and got out his notepad and pen. I could hear him speaking softly to the boy. The cameraman quickly took a white balance and did a sound check. I looked at the viewfinder to make sure that both my subjects were in the frame, and that the time code was visible in the picture.

'Ready?' I asked Jaafer-bhai.

He gave me a thumbs-up.

I turned to the cameraman. 'Okay, roll.'

A pause. 'Rolling.' The cameraman.

The boy cleared his throat. '*Maaru naam Mohammed Asif Shaikh chhe . . .*'

Jaafer-bhai began to write.

'Sunaaf?' he prompted.

'S . . . *Sunaaf?*'

'Father's name.'

The boy swallowed, then continued. 'Son of . . .'

'*What* is going on here!' Ramya's voice rang out from the doorway. 'Stop! *Cut!*'

'What's wrong?'

She pointed at the viewfinder. Turned and glared at the cameraman. 'You think this is a Bollywood film? *Who* told you to zoom the shot? You're not supposed to use your brain! Just frame it and leave it!'

I got up to look: the cameraman had zoomed in to a solo shot of the boy and excluded Jaafer-bhai from the frame.

'*Reframe!*' she ordered, storming out of the room. 'You have to start over again!' She paused, and turned with a baleful look at Jaafer-bhai. 'And *this* time keep it in Gujarati. No English, you hear?'

I stood with the cameraman while he set the frame again, wide enough that both Jaafer-bhai and the boy would always be fully visible.

'Okay,' I said. 'Whenever you are ready, Jaafer-bhai.'

He nodded.

I looked at the cameraman and he nodded. 'Another take?'

'No. Rewind and erase. This time, no cuts, no zooms and no retakes. We have to do the whole thing in a single take. Ready?'

Another pause. 'Rolling . . .'

3

Adil huddled with the other survivors on the Godhra platform, watching the adult passengers give their depositions about the fire in coach S6 to the police. By evening the police had taken down their statements, and they were free to leave if they wanted.

Some passengers had broken windows and jumped down seven feet to the ground, and a few of them had landed badly and fractured a leg. They were taken away for treatment. And burns: some passengers had minor burns on their face and top of their heads, and even on their shoulders. But the biggest cause of distress among the survivors was the toxic smoke: many people still had difficulty breathing. Their faces were covered in black soot, which was thickest around their nostrils.

Adil remembered the woman behind him in the line. The one who had fainted. She would not have survived. The carriage had burst into flames as soon as they had left.

He searched for a pay phone on the platform and called the school where his mother taught Urdu, to leave a message for her that he was safe and in Godhra station. She had known that he would be coming back by the Sabarmati Express. She would have been expecting him home by now. Maybe she had even heard about the fire on the train.

The dead bodies were brought out of the burnt carriage after it had cooled down, around half-past two. There were fifty-eight bodies. Some said fifty-nine. The doctors set up to do the autopsies in the railway yard and made fast work of it. By sunset they were done, and five trucks came and loaded the bodies to take to Ahmedabad.

As the story of the fire was told again and again to the police, Adil saw it growing into a conspiracy and a tale of arson. Some kar sevaks said in their depositions that they had seen burning rags being flung into the carriage. Mashals, they said, burning torches, hurled by the crowd of Muslims outside. One passenger said that something inflammable had been thrown into the toilet. And then they started to speak of intruders who had come into the carriage and thrown burning liquid onto the floor.

But Adil had not seen anything like that, nor had the passengers who were sitting near him. All he knew was that he had suddenly smelt acrid smoke that made him cough, and seen a seat nearby that seemed to be smouldering. By the time he had noticed the smoke, all he could think of was getting away, getting out of the carriage.

How had it started? He didn't know.

The three damaged coaches were detached from the train, and their passengers were offered the option of finding space in other carriages to continue the journey to Ahmedabad that evening. But by then Adil had had enough of the Sabarmati

Express, and of his travelling companions, particularly the kar sevaks.

And the men who had come for the bodies had filled him with fear.

A day of fire, he remembered his grandfather saying. On a day of fire, the ghosts will leave the graveyards and roam around among the living. They know that something bad is about to happen, and they want to be a part of it. They would come out of their graves at sunset.

And the bones of the dead . . .

And the bones of all the dead fishermen will rise up out of the waves, shining like coral, and dance upon the sand.

Adil decided then and there that he would spend the night in the station's musafir-khana, and travel to Ahmedabad the next morning by bus.

The bus journey from Godhra to Ahmedabad took six hours. Adil got down at the Geeta Mandir bus depot, and wondered whether to take an autoricksha home.

His first inkling that things were not right was when he saw the rick drivers refusing to go towards Jamalpur. They were saying it was not safe.

So he decided to walk.

He turned onto a lane rimmed with tiny brightly painted houses and headed straight for the Urdu school, hoping to meet his mother before he went home and got ready to go to his own school. But he found the street crowded with children, children milling around everywhere, all of them out of uniform, creating noise and commotion, roaming around in packs with barely any adults in sight.

As if they had taken over the streets.

As if it was a school holiday.

But it could not possibly be a school holiday. Adil had been rushing back to Ahmedabad on an overnight train only to be in time for school the next day. He had had a few days' break after his pre-Board exams, and he had gone to spend them with his maternal uncle. But his teachers had fixed three days of extra tuition classes for Thursday, Friday and Saturday. And today was Thursday. They would *not* have closed his school.

Adil noticed a procession of men coming towards him. His heart suddenly began to pound. The men who had come to Godhra at sunset to take away the corpses. Coming this time for him!

Ghouls . . . Nowhere to run . . .

'*Bhaiiiii!*'

Adil froze. Faiza.

'*Addie-bhai!!*'

Time stood still. Addie, he wondered. Why is she calling me Addie?

The men were coming closer.

'You!' one of them pointed at Adil. 'Addie!'

Adil blinked.

'That child is calling you. You can't hear? Your name is not Aditya?'

Adil nodded mutely.

There was a boy he knew called Aditya. A Hindu boy he had played cricket with. They had once joked that Addie would have been a good nickname for both of them. And he had told Faiza this.

Then Faiza appeared beside him. She was wearing trousers and a T-shirt that had once been her costume in a school play.

'*Thank* you, Uncle,' she said tremulously in English. She wrinkled her nose, pushing her glasses up higher, and turned to Adil. 'Addie-bhai,' she said in Gujarati, 'Mummy is looking for you. It is time to go to the station.'

Faiza's accent was different. Not like a Muslim girl.

Je Amdavaad ni Khadia pol ma Gujarati Nagar kanyaon bole te . . . The sort Gujarati Nagar Brahmin girls would speak in one of the Khadia neighbourhoods of Ahmedabad. Adil remembered his mother's description of the tinkling sweet sound of 'pure' Gujarati.

Faiza turned again to the ghoul. 'Sorry, Uncle,' she lilted, 'but he sometimes has fits, you know? Then he goes off by himself and we have to look for him.' She turned to Adil again. 'Come, let's go.'

He let her lead him away, and they turned back and headed towards the railway station.

'Faizoo . . .' he began softly.

'Not yet, Bhai,' she whispered. Her eyes were bright, and her whole body was tense and stiff. 'Don't say anything. They will hear.'

They walked in silence until they reached the end of the street and turned the corner. He put his arm around her. She was shaking.

'What is it, Faizoo? Now you can tell me.'

'I don't know, Bhai. But I'm so . . . *scared*. Something is going to happen. If . . .' she sniffed, 'if they got to know you were a Muslim, I don't know what they would have done to you.'

'What do you mean, Faizoo?'

'They know, Bhai. They can tell from how we speak that we are Muslims. I was praying that you wouldn't talk.'

'No-no! I meant: what is this all of a sudden? Why would they hurt me if they knew I was a Muslim? Something has happened?'

'No, but something bad is *going* to happen, Bhai,' she repeated softly. 'I can feel it. The Hindu people are looking at us like we are . . . bad. Or they don't want to look at us.'

'Because of . . .'

'Because of what happened to the train. Amma told me . . .'

Amma, he suddenly remembered. 'You said that she was calling me?'

'No, Bhai. It was just an excuse.' She sniffed, started again. 'Zafar-bhai went this morning to the station, when the train from Godhra came. In his autoricksha. And he told me there were lots and lots of goondas waiting for the train, and raising shlokas. So he came away fast.'

'Raising *slogans*.'

'Slogans. He said he didn't see you. So I thought something had happened to you!'

'I came by bus. Left this morning.' He paused. 'I was in that carriage, Faizoo. S6. The one that caught fire.'

'Oh *no!*'

'Yes,' he went on. 'The coach was full of Hindu goondas. They were coming back from Ayodhya. They were raising slogans on Godhra platform when we first stopped. Must have had a fight with a vendor. Then they ran back inside and locked the doors, closed up all the windows, the doors, everything. Because people from the platform wanted to get in. And they were pelting us with stones.'

'They said that Muslim people were throwing burning things into the carriage.'

'I didn't see that. I think all the windows were closed. And no one came inside. *No* one could get inside. There were bedrolls and luggage barricading the doors! And if they had, you think the goondas would have let them start a fire, and wait for it to catch?'

'So how did the fire start?'

'*That* I don't know. When I smelt the smoke, I just ran. Like everybody else.'

They took a shortcut through the back lanes and headed towards the old town. Adil looked back to see if the men were following them.

They weren't. The ghouls had staked out a house. One of them went up to the meter box and turned off the power supply to the building. Then they brought tanks of propane, cooking gas, and carried them inside.

'Why are they taking the tanks inside, Bhai?' she whispered.

An explosion, Adil thought. They were going to open the tanks and release all the gas into the house, and set it off with electrical sparks.

'I think they will turn on all the light switches inside the house,' he said softly. 'Then they will open the tanks to fill the house up with gas.'

'But . . .'

The men came back out and they both fell silent and watched. They brought out appliances and furniture, and a trunk, which they opened right on the street. They threw out the bright wedding clothes and rummaged inside to find the jewellery.

'That is Atiya-ben's dowry,' Faiza said softly. 'Her sister is in my class.'

Then the main ghoul looked at his watch, got up and headed for the meter box.

'Come away, Faizoo. It is going to blow up!'

He ducked into a doorway, pulling Faiza with him.

He looked out and saw the man switch on the mains again.

There was a sudden 'boom' and the building exploded, turned black. The steel girders burst forth from the concrete like hands held out in prayer.

Black smoke filled the sky.

'They came this morning,' Faiza said. 'In five trucks. With the bodies. All the people who died in the fire. They were taking them around everywhere in Ahmedabad, and showing them to people. "This is what the Muslims have done to us."'

'And they closed the schools?'

'They called a bandh, Bhai. They shut down the whole city.'

A bandh. All offices closed, all factories, all shops. And all schools. The ghouls were now free to roam among the living. And bad things had already begun to happen.

'Where is Amma, Faizoo?'

'I don't know, Bhai.'

'She must be at home.'

'I think we should go and look.'

They headed back to Jamalpur and turned into their lane. The buildings on their lane had been spared. Jamalpur was a mixed locality, with both Muslims and Hindus. Not a prime target for the goons.

Their ground floor flat had been broken into, and the trunk had been opened. The books were off the shelves and in piles on the floor.

But there was no sign of Amma.

'We can't stay here,' Adil decided. 'We should go somewhere safe.'

'Yes,' Faiza agreed. 'We will go to the train station, and come back later and wait here for Amma.'

They passed a line of Muslim homes on the old town side that had all been burnt.

They were about to cross to the other side of the road when they saw a car pull over and stop right next to them. The back door opened and a young woman got out. Her head was covered with a peach-coloured dupatta. Her eyes were golden-green, large and almond-shaped.

Like a cat's, Adil thought.

The girl looked at him and raised her eyebrows quizzically.

Adil realized with a start that he was staring. He quickly and respectfully averted his glance and fixed his eyes on a pothole at the side of the road.

The back door on the other side opened and another girl got out and joined her.

'We are . . . from SEWA,' the girl with the peach dupatta began hesitantly.

SEWA: Self-Employed Women's Association. A Gujarati

NGO that looked after the interests of poor working women, and sometimes of minority groups too.

But she didn't sound like a local: she wasn't even speaking to them in Gujarati. And she looked like a northerner. No, she couldn't really be from SEWA.

Maybe she was a journalist.

Then why had she said . . .

'We heard that there was violence in this colony,' she continued, halting Adil's train of thought. 'Someone told us that some of the houses here had been burnt.'

'I can show you,' Faiza volunteered. 'And I know how they did it. I saw them! Come!'

Adil turned and watched the two of them go inside one of the houses. The girl with the peach dupatta nodded as she listened to Faiza, and started writing down what she said in her notebook. He could hear Faiza expounding on exactly how the houses were blown up.

'And do you live in this area?' the girl asked.

'No-no, our house is in Jamalpur,' she pointed in the general direction.

'And the two of you are alone? What about . . .'

'We are actually looking for our mother. We don't know where she is.'

Adil followed them inside to join the conversation. He looked around at the blackened walls, at the places where the light switches had all melted, vaporized. There were holes in the wall where the burnt wiring showed through.

'Megha!' He suddenly heard the other girl's voice calling from outside.

Megha?

'Just a minute!' the girl called back in English. 'I'm almost done.'

Adil saw Faiza's jaw drop.

The girl named Megha looked up from her notepad and saw the stunned look on Faiza's face. For a moment she looked puzzled. Then she looked down. Like a small child caught out telling a lie? No. It was something else.

'It's all right,' Adil told her softly.

She looked at him for a long moment, then nodded. 'Thanks.' She turned to Faiza, 'Thank you for showing me, Faiza.'

Adil watched her walking away with her friend, who was following an old man. She was talking intently. He heard her friend saying 'sorry, sorry . . .'

Faiza's voice brought him back to Earth. 'Her name was Megha, Bhai. And I had thought she must be a Muslim. She was speaking to me in Urdu.'

'Yes.'

'But . . . did you see?' She paused. 'How she looked when . . . when she saw that I had heard her name?'

He nodded. Not just caught out in a small lie, he decided. She was embarrassed. Her eyes had darkened. Lost that lovely golden light. She had stepped back into herself. Decided to hurry up and leave. Shame?

'Bhai?'

Guilt. The word suddenly fell into place. He looked at the ruined houses all along the road. Maybe she had felt she was in some way *responsible* for all of this. And she must have come to try and make amends.

Megha, he thought. So that was her name!

'Why do you think she was speaking to me in Urdu, Bhai?'

Adil suddenly remembered where they were. 'I guess she was doing the same thing you did when you spoke to those goondas. You didn't want them to know we were Muslims. And maybe she didn't want anyone here to guess she was a Hindu. But her friend went and spoilt it.'

Faiza nodded. 'That was a bad thing her friend did. I wish she had stayed.'

'Me too.'

He turned and looked at her retreating back, saw her heading with her friend towards an angry-looking crowd. He watched her adjust her dupatta to hide her hair better. Then, out of nowhere, a rag-tag band of children appeared and quickly surrounded her, and began to follow her, chattering away gaily. As though she was the Pied Piper.

'Bhai . . .'

He turned and looked again at Faiza, remembering how she had appeared in the nick of time and saved him from the goons.

'You were really smart today, Faizoo. And brave.'

'When?'

'When you called me Addie-bhai.' They crossed the road away from the burnt houses and headed for the train station.

'Oh!'

'Yes. I didn't realize it then, but I think you might have saved my life.'

4

We all had chai after the recording, and sat together around the table feeling the afterglow of a successful shoot. Once the camera was off, the boys relaxed, quite ready now to go on with their tales of that day.

I asked the cameraman to make me a VHS copy of the master tape, so it could be played on a home VCR. The judge would also not be able to view the shooting tape without an editing machine – though we would offer the original too if she requested it. I told the cameraman to make sure that the time code was showing in the copy frame too.

Jaafer-bhai and Anoop had put away their notepads, and the pace of the telling shot up. I reckoned 120 words per minute. Maybe 125. A good few notches above the average speed of speech I had measured for Hindi. The boys were excited now, and they spoke with hardly any pauses. My two scribes would have keeled over if they had had to keep up with this torrent of words!

I tried to follow what they were saying. It wasn't difficult: some of those stories I had heard already. A friend of mine had gone and worked as a medic in the relief camps in Ahmedabad. And she had come back totally depressed.

Another round of chai and I looked at my watch. It was going on eleven.

The cameraman returned with the VHS tape and gave it to me along with the original. We all said our goodbyes and exchanged phone numbers, and promised to stay in touch. Then Jaafer-bhai, Anoop and I headed back up the stairs to the control room with the notepads and the videotapes.

'Jaafer-bhai, while it's all still fresh in your mind, I want you to go and transcribe your interview off the videotape. Neatly: as neatly as the cops wrote the confessions. Use the pause button, and rewind if you need to. This time no abbreviations, and no skipping. And no crossing out. I need every single word. Even the false starts.' I paused to stress this. '*Especially* the false starts and the unfinished sentences. We are going to look at those sentences later.'

'Right, Madam. Every word.'

'And note the exact time you start, and the exact time you end. And here,' I handed him a legal size notepad, 'write on this. Not on your small notepad. I want this transcription to look like the actual confessions.'

Anoop was sent off to work out the average number of words per sentence in each of the confessions, and the number of words in the longest sentence. And to tag any sentences that trailed off, or seemed to be unfinished.

I picked up the two small notepads and settled down in a comfortable chair, opened Jaafer-bhai's first. I couldn't read anything except for a few acronyms he had written in English. But it was all there.

Jaafer-bhai's handwriting had deteriorated badly by the

third page: it had become larger and more irregular, and the words were becoming shorter and shorter. He must be using abbreviations. Each line would start a little further away from the left margin, and the vowel maatras were all right-shifted, as his hand flew from left to right across the page. The same way a dot on an *i* or the crossing on a *t* would shift to the right if one were writing this fast in English. His tension showed in the way he kept making mistakes and scratching them out.

I counted the total corpus of words and divided it by the exact time he had taken.

Forty-six words per minute! So *that* was what forty-six words per minute looked like in Gujarati.

I paused to admire his work.

Anoop's handwriting was neater overall than Jaafer-bhai's, but he had clocked only forty words per minute.

Then I reached for the confession statement on my desk, from the youngest suspect, counted the words and did the same calculation.

Sixty words per minute.

Sixty! Did the bugger actually think he was writing at sixty words per minute?

I paused. No. The policeman who had written down the confession statement had just filled in what he felt looked like a credible amount of time to put down on a log. He had made a wild guess based on how long he imagined it would have taken if this were a real confession. He had absolutely no idea what his numbers meant in terms of a transcription speed. And he had never thought to compare his speed with anyone else's.

Luckily for us.

'Madam!' I heard Anoop's voice for the first time. 'Average number of words in sentence is thirty. Longest sentence seventy words.'

'Number of unfinished sentences?'

'No unfinished sentences, Madam. All complete.'

Crazy! I tried to conjure up an image of a voluble young militant, earnestly implicating himself to a stern Gujarati policeman in long, long sentences, one of them having no less than seventy words. All of which were complete and well formed.

And dictating it all at the lightning confessional speed of sixty words per minute!

'How is it going?' Ramya's voice over my shoulder.

I filled her in on the stupendous numbers we had got.

'Great!' she said. 'Just hope you can be this convincing in court.' She turned and frowned at Jaafer-bhai, busy in front of the VCR, one hand on the pause button. 'And what is *he* up to?'

'Just an idea I got after I saw one of the confessions. To try to calculate the *real* speed of a transcription as neat as that. Might be a useful figure to have. I'm getting him to take down the full testimony off the tape. Then I can compare that with what he wrote on camera. I got the impression that he was skipping bits, towards the end. He must have been tired . . .'

'I'll order coffee for him. For you too?'

I took a coffee break and waited for Jaafer-bhai to finish.

The language, I thought. I needed Jaafer-bhai's instincts

about the language. Anoop would not do: he was not Muslim. But Jaafer-bhai would be able to tell at once if the language of the confession sounded in any way different from the words a young Muslim boy would have used.

I had done something like this before. Back in'84, at the time of the anti-Sikh violence in Delhi. Found a way to assess the communal flavour of a text numerically.

I dug into my handbag and found a red ballpoint pen. There was a blue one next to it. I took that out too.

Soon Jaafer-bhai turned off the VCR and stood up. He came over to my desk and with a flourish set down an immaculate-looking piece of transcription.

It was longer than the one he had done on camera. The words were longer, and the entire text looked longer too. He hadn't used his judgement and edited out false starts and repetitions. And, like the confession, each line of the transcription was perfectly aligned to an imaginary margin.

I counted the corpus of words and calculated his speed of transcription: eighteen words per minute.

'*Fantastic!*' I beamed. 'Thank *you*, Jaafer-bhai!'

I signalled to Anoop to come over, and handed him Jaafer-bhai's transcription. 'Can you do the same analysis for this? Average length of sentences, length of longest sentence, and tag the incomplete ones?'

'No problem.'

The youngest suspect's confession was still on my desk. I handed it to Jaafer-bhai, along with the red ballpoint pen. 'You have to use your instincts now. About the language. I want you to take this red pen and underline any words and phrases that look like something a policeman would say, but not a young Muslim boy. Please be careful where you start to underline and where you stop: we are going to count the words later.' I picked up the blue ballpoint pen. 'And take this blue pen. Underline any words and phrases that a Muslim boy would use but definitely not a policeman.'

Anoop brought me the results for Jaafer-bhai's transcription. The average number of words per sentence was just a shade below fourteen. The longest sentence had thirty-one words. There were five sentences tagged with a little dot, four of them near the beginning and one later on in the text. These would be the incompletes.

This was more like a confession, I thought. In every way: except for the neatness of the handwriting.

No, I suddenly saw. There was something unreal in the very idea of a confession. There could be no such thing as a natural flow of speech, if the suspect had to slow down to a dictation speed. Unless the suspect had experience in giving dictation to a secretary, there would have to be a lot of condensing of the actual information. There would be editorial judgement on the part of the *scribe*, or the police mediator present at the time of confession, as to what part of the overflow to keep and what to skip – if neatness was what mattered most. All of which *should* adversely affect the speed at which the confession could be taken.

Editing and paraphrasing. Could a paraphrase truly count as a verbatim confession?

Jaafer-bhai's transcription off the videotape, with his hand on the pause button, was an unreal specimen. Just like the bogus confessions we were busy analyzing here, penned by cops who had all the time in the world. It was the other transcription he had done on camera, in real time, that was actually the best one could hope to get, rough as it was. And even there, the boy had deliberately slowed down, and lengthened his pauses, to make it easier for Jaafer-bhai to take dictation. The boy had not been hostile.

I tried to clear my head. What had I been thinking?

A willing confession from a hostile suspect was an oxymoron. The suspect would simply not be able to preserve his equanimity while dictating words that would condemn him to a long prison sentence, or even to execution. He might sign the document under duress, under torture, knowing what it contained. But unless he was actually one of those obsessive-compulsives that the police have learnt to ignore, who are driven to show up in police stations and incriminate themselves in confessions, there was no way he could actually participate in framing this sort of confession statement.

'Madam, it is done.' Jaafer-bhai's voice brought me back to reality, to the room we were in, in Ahmedabad. To a world where fourteen young men had been sitting in jail these last three years, awaiting a trial that hinged on these confessions. 'I have underlined where suspect is talking like police.'

I took the confession statement from him. There were a few red underlines on each page, indicating use of alien terminology. There was nothing underlined in blue: at no time did the policeman writing the confession use a Muslim turn of phrase that might have been unfamiliar to him.

'In fact, whole thing does not sound like such a boy,' he said. 'Here is saying dharam guru. Muslim boy never say maulvi, maulana as dharam guru: may be not knowing that word!' He shook his head, pointed. 'But this part is worst.'

He pointed to a paragraph.

'What does that say?'

Jaafer-bhai cleared his throat. 'Boy is saying "prayaschit". This word coming in so many confessions. Means saying sorry. Is Sanskrit word. I never *hear* such a word before I read in confessions.'

'Deepa-ben . . .'

I turned and saw one of the young lawyers standing there.

'This is Apoorva-bhai, Madam. Lawyer.'

Apoorva-bhai nodded. 'Let me explain. He is right: not just this word, but this whole paragraph appears in all the confessions. Word for word, without any difference in punctuation. What is strange is that these boys were arrested and produced in two batches, so the confessions were not even taken on the same day. Or by the same scribe. Yet . . . this identical paragraph is there at the same place in, I think, all of them.'

'What does the paragraph say?'

'It is supposed to be an explanation for why there is this delay in admitting to the offence: that they were being dissuaded by their families. But that they are speaking now as . . . penance.'

'Atonement?'

'That is the word I was looking for. They are speaking to atone for what they have done. All the boys in each batch saw the light at exactly the same time, and in exactly the same words and with exactly the same punctuation.'

'Thanks! This is the most damning thing we have got all night!'

'And something else . . .' he hesitated. 'What is strange is that there is no rambling at all. Every confession, supposedly verbatim, only goes straight for the stuff that would implicate the suspect. Nothing else is mentioned. At all.' He shook his head. 'And the scribe could not be using his judgement and skipping out irrelevant information: it would show as more time taken.'

I nodded. Better and better.

Apoorva-bhai turned back to the first page. 'In the first part of the confession, in the scribe's words, there is this sentence: "*Tamara qaboolat-nama levaama avechhe.*" Means: your confession is being *taken*. Shouldn't it instead be: *given*? Willingly?'

'No!' I perked up at once. 'I see something else here! *Taken* is a confirmation that this is all supposedly being done in real time. Something I have been assuming here. From the existence of a log. But this is the proof! "Taken" here means "taken *down*". By the scribe. Or by the police. They have said it in so many words!'

A guffaw from Jaafer-bhai caught my attention.

'Madam! Look!' Jaafer-bhai stood at his desk with a confession in his hand. He held it by a top corner and flipped the bottom right corner. The lines were in perfect registration.

'Madam, you have seen those cartoon books? Where you turn a page and then the next is almost the same in the corner?' He picked up the confession and flipped it again.

'A flipbook!' I exclaimed. 'It's almost like an animation flipbook!'

I remembered a wry comment a cartoonist friend had made about a book: the story is okay, but does it *flip*? This one definitely did!

'Yes,' said Apoorva-bhai, 'every page ends in exactly the same place. Isn't that a bit strange? I mean, this is unlined paper. Wouldn't the scribe just, you know, end each page when he reached the end of the sentence? Instead of turning the page mid-sentence? And how would he have got it so exact?'

'Same way Disney did it,' I replied. 'By tracing. Keeping the next sheet on top of the one he had just done. Each image has to be consistent with the earlier one. This scribe was so bored that he amused himself by keeping the lines in registration. No *way* is this a verbatim confession!' I leapt to my feet and looked around for a computer. 'I'm going to start writing up a summary of all this. When you . . .' I looked at Anoop and Jaafer-bhai, 'when *you* have the numbers, I'll add them in.'

Ramya called a pack-up at 4 a.m., and we all trooped down the stairs to the basement, and into the hotel's dark twenty-four-hour cafe. We joined some tables together, and someone went and woke up a waiter in the kitchen.

We asked him what there was to eat. He reeled off a list of standard north Indian fare.

Great, I thought. I come all the way to Ahmedabad, and all I get to eat is bad north Indian food!

Ramya caught my expression. 'Don't worry, we'll find

something better for lunch tomorrow. We only have to be in court in the afternoon.'

'When?'

'Not before four,' she said. 'We're going to the Sabarmati jail. The first hearing is going to be in the jail itself. Thought you'd get a kick out of that.'

5

Violence is a nasha, thought Vijay, as he strode down the dark empty street.

A high. Just like speed. Just like money.

Like power.

The sound of his footsteps echoed back at him from the burnt-out frames of the houses he passed.

In normal times we cannot give in to this urge. There are rules. There are notions of civilized behaviour.

He turned the corner into a dark narrow lane.

But then there are those rare moments when all the rules go up in smoke. And we are told that it is all right to be brutal: in fact, that it is good. Then the beast within us opens its eyes.

A stray dog looked up as he passed, made eye contact.

That is not my nasha, he returned to his mental soliloquy. In his mind's eye he could see the bottle of Royal Stag whisky waiting for him in his cupboard at home, hidden from public view because of the prohibition that was the last hangover from Gandhi-ji.

Infinitely more appealing.

He shook his head. No, I don't have what it takes to go out there and hurt people. And enjoy it.

The dog put its head down, went back to sleep.

He thought of the times when a little ruthlessness, a bit of killer instinct would have served him well in his work. When he could have fought. Got even. Not thought of the damage it would cause to a colleague. Not cared.

He was no stranger to violence. But for him it had always been reactive. He had never been the instigator. And he had not *enjoyed* the blows that he had landed.

Today had been a revelation. For the first time ever, the middle class had joined in the orgy of violence, turning on their own neighbours. Until now, they had always held back, and left the dirty work to the real foot soldiers. The poor. And the tribals.

Something had changed today. Maybe it had been building up for a long time. Women, middle class women, had gone up and garlanded the men in the mobs, treated them as heroes. Before they even had a chance to reflect, or regret what they had done.

The urge to bully must run deep in the human spirit, he decided. Much deeper than one would think. The urge to seek out people who were weaker, helpless, and beat them to a pulp. All it needed was a chance to come out.

He passed the last of the burnt buildings and left the old city behind him, passed the bus terminal and headed towards Jamalpur Darwaza.

Allah o Akbar! Allaaaaaah o Akbar!

The azaan, coming from Jamalpur mosque, near the river. The last call to prayer for the day.

Allah o Akbar! Allaaaaaah o Akbar!

It sounded clear tonight, Vijay thought. Clearer than ever. He felt he could hear every word distinctly. I've been hearing this sound every day for so many years, he suddenly realized. And yet I have no idea what it means.

The sound kept him company as he walked. He had to admire the resolve of the old moazzin, going ahead with the azaan even on a tense night like this.

The last reverb of sound, and then silence again. He could hear his feet striking the paved road in a steady rhythm.

'Sir!'

Something must have spooked one of his men.

He turned back, lifted his eyebrows: what?

'Some strange noise is coming from that place!' The policeman took out his service revolver and, with a click, released the safety catch. He pointed the gun at the door of a dark house. 'Hands up! Come out!'

There was the sound of bare feet slapping the stone floor, and a little girl about ten or eleven years old came and peeked out the doorway. Behind her glasses, her eyes were wide with fright. Her hands were cupped in front of her. She had been reciting the namaaz.

She came out onto the street and lifted her hands slowly above her head.

'It's a child,' Vijay said tiredly. 'Put that gun away.'

Then an older boy appeared in the doorway, lifting his hands above his head.

'No, sir. There are more of them. They may be armed!'

'Anyone else in the house?' Vijay called out to them.

'No, Uncle,' the little girl replied. 'Just the two of us. We are waiting for our mother to come back.'

Vijay sighed. How many innocent children were waiting like this tonight?

'Do you know that this locality is under curfew?' he asked gently.

She nodded. 'But we were inside. The curfew is only for outside, isn't it?'

Vijay turned to his men. 'Continue to patrol,' he ordered, waving them ahead. He turned back to the two children. 'Come here. Tell me your names.'

The little girl gulped. 'My name is Faiza Ansari.' She turned her head to indicate her brother. 'And my brother's name is Adil. Are we under arrest?'

Vijay suppressed a smile. 'No, but I have to take you with me. You can't stay here. It's not safe.' A thought struck him. 'Have you had anything to eat?'

'No, Uncle, but it's okay.'

'How long have you been waiting here?'

'We came back here last evening,' the boy supplied. His sister turned and gave him a cross look.

'Then you had better come with me,' Vijay insisted.

'Our mother . . .'

'She won't come home tonight. There is a curfew.'

Many of the people had fled the locality, he knew. They would have taken refuge in Shah Alam dargah, a sufi shrine a few kilometres south of Jamalpur.

The little girl looked uncertain.

'She can't come tonight,' he insisted.

'She would still try, I think. She would be worrying about us.'

'No. Not tonight. She would not be allowed on the street.'

The little girl hesitated a moment, then wagged her head in agreement. She went back into the house to slip on her shoes, signalling to her brother to do the same.

'Come Bhai,' she said. 'I think it's okay.'

They returned a moment later with a little bundle, a change of clothes.

'Come, let's go,' Vijay repeated. 'Tomorrow . . . tomorrow we will go and find your mother.'

6

A doorbell rang. Adil opened his eyes.

He was in a dimly lit room. There was a soft pillow under his head, and a thick cotton quilt around him. He reached out a hand and touched the cold floor.

A door opened. Two sets of footsteps came back into the room.

Adil closed his eyes, pretended to be asleep.

'Your son?' he heard an older man say.

'No, sir. We have no children as yet.'

The policeman who had taken them both home. Whose wife had fed them dinner, and then taken Faiza with her to sleep in the bedroom. Leaving him and the policeman to sleep in the living room.

The clink of ice cubes against a glass. The scrape of a chair against the floor.

'I found him while patrolling Jamalpur tonight. And his sister. They were waiting for their mother all alone in their house. Their neighbours were gone.' A pause. 'They hadn't had anything to eat since the night before. And they seemed to be from a good family. Educated people.'

'Cheers.' The older man's voice.

A long silence. Adil felt himself drifting off to sleep.

'Vijay . . .'

Adil was suddenly alert.

'He called us for a meeting that night.'

'I heard about it, sir. We get to know.'

'Then you know that they planned the bandh. To allow the riots to happen.'

'We knew we were not supposed to interfere.' A pause. 'The first morning they had some disturbances. In a few localities. Small things. We knew it was a test, to see if we would interfere or not. When they saw that the police were not going to make trouble for them, they started the real riots. That afternoon.'

Another pause. 'There was no need to bring those bodies to Ahmedabad, Vijay. They should have kept this thing in Godhra. Now they will not be able to control it.'

A long pause. 'I can't understand the need for riots at all!' Vijay growled.

'The riots? You know why riots like this happen.' A pause. 'Yes, here.'

A chair scraping the floor. Ice cubes tumbling into a glass.

'Bas, Vijay. Thanks. We all know it has nothing to do with little people and centuries of dushmani. No. It is much simpler. Much more cold-blooded than that.'

'I know it is not about little people. What is it this time?'

'They knew they were going to lose the elections. Already they had lost the panchayat elections. And two by-elections. Nothing was working. There was only one thing left to try.'

'The communal card . . .'

'And then this thing happened. In Godhra. He didn't even have to make it up.'

A pause. 'Be careful, sir. If they think you are going to talk . . .'

'What will they do?'

'They will kill you. I know their mood. They are capable of it.'

'I haven't said anything. Yet.' A pause. 'And I am not some small Muslim in the street who they can snuff out and no one will say a word. They will think a thousand times before they do anything to me.' Another pause. 'And what about you? You don't have a reason to worry? It doesn't show on your face that you think you are better than them?'

A long silence.

'I don't think . . .' Vijay began.

'Come on, Vijay. Cut out the useless talk. These men are insecure little people. And one thing that they cannot stand is someone who reminds them how small they are. Someone with confidence.' He laughed. 'You know what they call you people? Pseudo-secularists. Not good Hindus. Always making friends with the minorities. You think they give a damn about whether you do pujas in the house? No! What makes them crazy is that you don't need *them*. The way they need each other.'

A sudden scurry of little feet on the stone floor. Little claws skritch-scratching as they went. Adil opened his eyes and found himself face-to-face with a medium-sized mouse that had paused to consider him.

A burst of laughter and the mouse took off and hid itself behind a cabinet. Adil shut his eyes again.

'If you could only see your face now, Vijay! I can just read your mind!' A pause. 'You know, if there is one thing these little people hate more than Muslims, it is secularists. At the end of the day, they can do business with Muslims. With the leaders. All religious fundamentalists understand each other, want the same things.' A pause. The sound of ice cubes swirling in a glass. 'But it is people like you that they are most suspicious of. "Secularists should be deported to Pakistan."'

'I have heard that. My family has enough of those types.'

'And they all feel this way about you,' the older man ended the sentence for him. 'They will support you, when all the chips are down, because you are family. But they don't feel comfortable with you.'

'No.'

'Because you are different. They see your stance in this thing as contempt for their values. Contempt for who they are.'

'"We don't agree with you on your choice of friends." That is how they put it. As if it was only something to do with personal taste . . .'

'Maybe it is.'

'No. This kind of brutality has nothing to do with "taste". I went out today and saw what they had done, after they let me out of the office. Bodies all over the streets. Stabbed. Burnt.' Another pause. 'And there is nothing spontaneous about this. They were going around with lists. They *knew*. They knew which flat had Muslims living in it! Where did these lists come from? They were just waiting for a chance to do this!'

'You misunderstand me, Vijay . . .'

'And they *knew* which shops belonged to Muslims. Even I don't know this! How can you tell? The shops all have Hindu names. Or English names. But they knew!'

'Vijay. What I meant is that it *is* a sort of personal taste. You are not just some hero trying to be good. That is not your main motivation. No, hear me out . . .' A pause. 'Sometimes I think you secularists are like a special sort of Brahmin. You don't have to go out there and get your hands dirty, and slog for your daily bread. You can sit back and be abstract. Take a Devil's Advocate view of things. And like a Brahmin, it comes easily to you to look down on the little people. You worry about the minorities, yes. But what you are seeing is not *people*. It is causes. And between you and the people you want to help is the great big mass in the middle. Not People Like Us.'

'Be careful using the word "abstract" like that, sir. It is abstract thinking that allows a man to attack a perfect stranger, just because he is told the man is a Muslim. Or a Christian.'

'There is enough violence among those people you call non-abstract thinkers.'

'Yes, but they are small fights. Face to face. And mostly between equals. But when the thinking becomes abstract, you do not have a fight. Then you have a riot.' A pause. 'They are using the word riot. I would have used another word.'

'Which is?'

'Pogrom. A word for violence directed against a minority group. And supported by the State.'

A long pause.

'How are you different, sir? Aren't you a special sort of Brahmin too?'

'Me? No, Vijay. Not a special sort of Brahmin. I am just an ordinary Brahmin. A Party man, concerned about what this is doing to the Party. And concerned about the little people there in the middle who are lapping this up now, and who are beginning to believe that this is their fight. They believe that they are actually the ones out there doing these things, when, in truth, they are at home quaking with fear, and worried about damage to their property.' A pause. 'My constituents. I am worried about what this is doing to the people who voted for me.'

'An ordinary Brahmin with a conscience . . .'

'Yes, a conscience.' The sound of a glass put down on a wooden table. 'Chal, Vijay. Avje. I'll make a move.'

Footsteps receding. A door closed.

An ordinary Brahmin with a conscience . . .

The words rang in Adil's mind as he drifted back to sleep.

7

'They've got a special court recorder for you. The best they have – for taking down testimony in English,' Ramya said, as we stepped out of the little vegetarian eatery onto the pavement.

A herd of cows was making its way towards us. They took up the full width of the pavement. Gujarati cows had the biggest horns I had ever seen on cows anywhere. Some were a good two feet long. And with their narrow faces and heavy-lidded eyes, they looked a lean-mean bunch. I stepped onto the road to let them pass.

I knew they were vegetarians. Herbivores, in fact. But that wasn't the point. They could lose it and take it into their heads to charge. A friend's son had once been chased by an angry bull on the streets of Ahmedabad. He had had to climb a wall and sit it out, waiting for the beast to move on.

We stopped a rick and got in. Ramya told the driver to take us to the Sabarmati jail.

'You were saying something about a court recorder?' I remembered.

'Yes. Since you are going to depose in English, and they

know you are a linguist, they have gone and got you the best man they have.'

The best! 'What would his name be?'

'Some Verma.'

'Yay!' I exulted. 'My lucky day!'

Ramya gave me a puzzled frown.

'Verma . . . Means he's from the same community as me. I want to get to know him better!'

I remembered my grandfather once bringing out our family tree, and showing it to me with pride. It went back to the court of the Emperor Aurangzeb. Our earliest known ancestor had worked as a scribe in his court.

I had told this to my best friend in school, but she had sneered. It seemed that she was from an even more elite line of Kayasths. *Her* earliest ancestor, she insisted, had been none other than the great Birbal himself. The Emperor Akbar's chief advisor, known for his wit and ingenuity. A full century before the time of Aurangzeb.

Her family had already been literate, and taking down testimony and confessions in the royal courts, while we were still swinging by our tails in the trees outside.

Along with Mr Verma's family.

Ramya and I stepped into the yard of the Sabarmati jail and we settled down on a bench to wait in the late afternoon sun. Across the lawn, white geese strutted in an orderly line and disappeared around the corner of the building. I looked up into the trees and saw that evolution had not taken me as far away from my ancestors as I had imagined.

The sun headed for the horizon.

'Isn't it getting late?' I asked.

'Not your problem,' Ramya replied dryly. 'Let's see. Still time.'

The sun was about to set by the time we were called into the courtroom. I stood a moment in the doorway and let my eyes adjust to the dimmer indoor light.

We had entered by a side door at the back of the courtroom. I walked toward the central aisle, turned right and approached the bench. Ramya manoeuvred me to a place on the left, just below the judge's seat.

The judge reminded me a bit of my grandmother. She had the attractive features of a well-bred older woman who had not had too much reason to doubt the values she had grown up with. *Suljhe-hue log*, the Hindi expression suddenly surfaced in my mind. Sorted-out folk. No rough edges. But fair, I thought. Like my grandmother. If I did not clash with her, she might listen to me, out of curiosity.

But when I rested my eyes on Mr Verma, a warbling Raj Kapoor-era soundtrack faded on in the background. It was the tune of a Turkish song, about a lady and a kaatib, a court scribe, and how on a journey together they fall in love. Mr Verma was wearing a bandh-gala, high-necked like the jacket the kaatib in the song was wearing.

I smiled.

'Yes, proceed,' the judge said gently.

'Your Honour, I call as my witness Dr Deepa Sahai, a linguist who will give her assessment of the confessional statements.'

'And you swear to tell the truth,' the judge added.

'Yes. I do.' I turned to Mr Verma. 'Since my deposition is going to be largely about the work of scribes, and my testimony is going to be written down in real time, I would like to be introduced to the court recorder.'

Mr Verma finished writing down my words and sat up, looked at me solemnly. 'Myself H.C. Verma. Court recorder.'

I looked back at him and nodded.

'Could you summarize for the court your qualifications and previous experience?' Ramya asked.

'I have a Ph.D in linguistics from the University of Pennsylvania.'

'USA,' the judge added, for the benefit of the court recorder.

'Yes. My first project after I got my doctorate involved assigning numerical scores to recorded speech. At that time, I developed a way of determining if the person I had recorded was a native speaker of the language by counting instances of certain features in their speech. And the overall speed.'

'And you have worked on confessional statements before?' The judge.

'Yes. I have. I did a similar analysis to what I am doing now in another POTA case, in Delhi. That also involved confessions.'

'Can you summarize your findings about the present confessions for the court?' Ramya again.

'Okay. For comparison purposes, I first did video recordings of two boys similar to the defendants making depositions to two professional scribes. The videotape is here with me and I will submit it to the court. It is unedited: the unbroken time code will confirm that.' I paused, turned to Mr Verma. 'What

I wanted to see was how a scribe, like *you*, takes down verbatim testimony: what happens to handwriting under pressure, what speed you are able to maintain. What adjustments the speaker giving the testimony has to make to accommodate you.' I paused again. 'The videotape shows two ideal confessional situations: the speakers in both cases were fully cooperative.'

'And what were your findings?' Ramya.

'One of our scribes was able to maintain a speed of forty-six words per minute. That is an extremely good speed, probably the highest I've seen in my experience with scribes. The other scribe was able to maintain forty words per minute.' I looked up at the judge. 'The videotape will confirm the duration of the two interviews. I just had to add up the total number of words and divide by the number of minutes.'

'Can you tell the court the purpose of the video recording?' Ramya.

'Yes. I wanted an ideal confessional statement for comparison purposes. Then I calculated the transcription speed of the actual confessions by counting the words and using the time log the police transcriber had recorded.'

'And your findings?' Ramya.

'The transcription speeds of the confessional statements averaged about sixty words per minute.' I paused, shuffled some papers. 'I have the breakdown here for each of the confessional statements.' I looked up at Mr Verma again. 'I think you would agree that such a speed is unrealistic.'

Mr Verma kept writing without looking up.

I let the silence hang a moment before I went on. Mr Verma looked up from his notepad gratefully.

'What was unrealistic was not just the overall speed. If you take a look at the transcription done by our scribe at forty-six words per minute . . .' I took out Jaafer-bhai's notebook, and the photocopy we had made of his notes to submit to the court, 'you will see that when a scribe writes at that speed, there is an expected pattern of distortions. I have listed them: handwriting becomes larger, words become shorter, significant use of abbreviations, each line on the page increasingly right-shifts away from the margin, maatras above and below letters also right-shifted, a certain number of scratches on the page . . .' I looked up again. 'I looked for signs of these features in the confessions: they are not there at all. The confession statements are all spectacularly neat and clean.'

I sent a blessing to all the class teachers who had taught the police scribes to keep their work neat. And to write in full sentences.

I held up a copy of a confession, turned the pages slowly, pointing to the last line on each page.

'I was also struck by the way each page ends in exactly the same place. Almost like an animation flipbook! Since the paper is unlined, and the scribe is not obliged to end each page in any particular spot, I would have expected there to be some unevenness here. I would have expected the transcription on some pages to end lower down than on others. It would have been normal for the scribe to have finished a sentence and *then* turned the page. Especially if he was writing fast.' I shook my head. 'Instead I get the sense of the scribes being more concerned with the *look* of the document. The neatness.' I looked up at the judge. 'Even when we *type*, many of us like to end a page at the end of a sentence. When it isn't necessary at all.'

I paused. Mr Verma turned a page.

'The only time when a scribe is not driven mostly by considerations of meaning is when the scribe is actually *copying* down the text. When the material already exists in written form.' I paused for effect. 'When the *confession* already exists in written form.' Another pause. 'Written, as opposed to verbatim.'

I caught Apoorva-bhai's smile out of the corner of my eye. Sent him and Jaafer-bhai a mental thank you for the insight about flipbooks.

'I also had a look at the language of the confessions. In verbatim testimony, there are bound to be a number of sentences that go nowhere, sentences which simply trail off. Or are crudely joined to what follows. I wanted to check . . .'

'Can you explain what you mean?' The judge.

'Yes. Often when we talk we . . . you know? Then we start again.' I looked up at Mr Verma. 'Mr Verma, could you read back my last sentence?'

Mr Verma cleared his throat. 'Often when we talk we, you know, then we start again.'

He was good!

'That is an example of it: a sentence that trailed off, and was badly joined to what followed.' I looked at the judge. 'Actually, fluency is mostly illusion. I don't believe we know when we start a sentence how we plan to end it. We are just good at smoothening the joints, making the sentences look planned. But when we are under pressure, or when we simply don't care, the jumps begin to show. I was able to . . . When I needed to show such an example, I could produce one with no effort.'

'Did you find any instances of these?' Ramya.

'Well, we managed to tag five incomplete sentences in the transcript copied off the videotape, four towards the beginning, and one later on. But the actual confessions had no such false-start sentences. Every sentence was complete and well-formed.'

'And what is surprising about that?' The judge.

'Well, I could see that happening if the speaker was experienced and in a position to take time and be careful. And if the sentences were relatively short. But the sentences in the confessions were *not* short.' I paused, shifted focus. 'In the transcript off the videotape, the average sentence was slightly less than 14 words in length, and the longest sentence was 31 words. Normal, I would say. Maybe even short.' I looked up at the judge. 'But that was where we got all the examples of incomplete sentences!'

'How long were the sentences in the confessions?' Ramya.

'In the first confession we studied, the average sentence length was around thirty words, and the longest sentence had as many as seventy words. The other confessions had similar word counts.' I shook my head. 'Even in literary text, when the writer has all the time in the world to go back and tinker with the language, such long sentences would be unusual. And this is meant to be verbatim testimony.'

I paused to let this sink in.

'In an earlier case, long back, I had to develop a way of

analyzing verbal content numerically,' I went on, shifting gears to a new subject. 'I would underline the words and phrases that were communally inappropriate in the text, count them and calculate them as a percentage of the total corpus.' I paused for breath. Mr Verma paused too. 'As these confessions are in Gujarati, I asked one of our scribes, who is from the same community as the boys, to underline the words and phrases that a Muslim boy would not use, but which a policeman would. And vice versa: any words or phrases that are typically Muslim, but which would have been alien to a Hindu policeman.'

'And what were your findings?' Ramya.

'In the mock confession, taken on video, a bit under 5 per cent of the text consisted of typically Muslim usage. There were no instances of typical police usage.'

Ramya nodded.

'In the actual confessions it was the opposite: about 3 per cent of the text consisted of police words or highly Sanskritized words that I would not expect the suspects to use, or maybe to even know. And there were no instances of typically Muslim usage.' I frowned, looked at the judge. 'You can take a look at the phrases that have been underlined. We have not done a content analysis of the confessions. I wanted to keep my observations at the level of numbers.'

The judge nodded approvingly. 'Good.'

'However, there is one paragraph my colleagues pointed out to me. This same paragraph occurs at about the same point in all the confessional statements: the same wording, the very same punctuation. Regardless of the scribe taking the confession, and regardless of the day on which the confession was being taken. It is a block paragraph that centres around the notion of atonement: prayaschit. This is a Sanskrit word that Muslim boys would probably not know. In fact, I don't know too many young men, Muslim or otherwise, who would ever use that word. It seems to me that it has been inserted into the document for purely legal purposes: to account for why the suspect did not admit to the offence at the time of arrest, but is suddenly doing so at the time of confession.' I paused for breath. Turned to look at Apoorvabhai.

He nodded.

'Another thing unusual in the confession, given that it is supposed to represent verbatim testimony, is the abnormal degree of *focus* in the confession. At no time does the testimony digress from material that would incriminate the suspect.'

I paused. Waited for Mr Verma to catch up.

'This is abnormal, in verbatim testimony. There *has* to be a degree of rambling. An expected amount of irrelevant material offered. This is not attested at all.'

'Perhaps the scribe omitted those bits?' the judge suggested. 'Court recorders are supposed to do this, you know.'

'He couldn't have. Given the extremely high speed of the scribe, sixty words per minute at an average, there could have been no time for editing or condensation of the material. Because any rejected testimony would have brought down the writing speed. The scribe himself has certified that this confession was being taken down in real time.' I pointed to the words in the first paragraph that confirmed this.

'To get back to the speed of writing,' the judge broke in, 'is it not possible that a scribe *could* have managed to write down a confession at that speed in Gujarati? I think Gujarati is a faster language to write than Hindi. Maybe your experience with Hindi . . .'

Papa, I suddenly remembered. This was why I had called him up.

'It *is* faster writing Gujarati,' I agreed. 'But not that much faster. In olden times, when scribes took down testimony in courts in this part of India, they would not use the modern Gujarati script that we are seeing in these confessions. They found it too slow for their purposes. They used another script . . .' I broke off. 'Your Honour, I come from a family of scribes too. We had our own script. It was based on Devanagari, but it was written running hand, like Urdu, only left-to-right. It was called Kaithi.'

Mr Verma nodded sagely.

'And it was used in Gujarat too?'

'No, Your Honour. There was a different script that scribes used in Gujarat and Maharashtra. For taking confessions.'

'And what was the name of this script?'

I took a deep breath. 'Modi,' I said out clearly. 'The name was Modi.'

There was an electric silence in the courtroom. As though I had just woken up a rattlesnake.

I learnt later from Papa that I had got the pronunciation wrong. He had simply spelt out the word for me, as I had asked. But a 'd' could be pronounced two ways in Hindi and Gujarati: what Papa had meant was the other 'd'. But no one in the courtroom knew that.

Except, perhaps, Mr Verma, who kept his eyes on his notebook.

I paused and savoured the charge in the air.

'What is your conclusion?' Ramya now. The all-important bottom line.

'My conclusion is that these confessions could not have been taken down in the manner in which the police have claimed. I am saying that there is serious doubt about the genuineness of these confession statements.'

I handed the videotape and the copies of the transcripts to the judge and we wound up shortly after. As I turned to go, I noticed that there were iron bars all along the back wall of the courtroom. I hadn't seen them when I came in.

Like in jail cells!

All of a sudden, a young man I didn't know, maybe twenty years old, rushed towards me out of the darkness on the other side of the bars, gripping them with his large, strong hands. He was smiling at me.

'*Thank* you, Ma'am!' I heard him say.

Then other young men also rushed forward, all smiling.

'Thank you, Ma'am,' the chorus went.

Ma'am?

My mind scrolled back to a class I had had just a week ago. My students had all written term papers, and I was handing them back, with grades. They had done well, and the grades reflected it. And they were beaming. Thank you, Ma'am . . .

'Ma'am!' The young man's voice called me back to the present. 'I am Adil. We all want to thank you for helping us!'

Adil! The youngest suspect!

Up to now he had existed only as a few pages of Photostat paper! I stopped and stared up at him. A bit taller than I had imagined. Warm brown eyes in a warm tanned face. Under his beard his features were smooth and regular.

So *this* was what he looked like.

'Come,' said Ramya, moving me on. 'We have a flight to catch.'

I did not want to let go of this moment. I held on to that one thing we both wanted . . .

'Don't give up,' I told him. 'We will win this case!'

'Inshallah . . .' someone in the group murmured.

He smiled, nodded. 'Let us hope . . .'

8

The judge handed her briefcase to a clerk, walked out of the courtroom and made her way towards the main entrance of the Sabarmati jail. She stepped out from under the arch and looked up a moment at the night sky. The stars were already out. Her car was waiting for her in the courtyard, and she got in the back and took her things from the clerk.

'Home,' she instructed the driver.

She looked out the window as he drove and tried to empty her mind. A stray image stuck, of the boys rushing forward and smiling through the bars at the last witness as she was leaving the courtroom, and of her surprise as she finally connected their faces with the testimony she had just given about their confessions.

Then she banished that image too. Sat back. The night was not over yet. Pooja-ben might already be there, waiting for her. She had sounded desperate when they had talked in the morning.

It must be her husband again.

The judge thanked her stars that she herself had managed to resist the pressure to get married. Now, at last, she was old enough that her family had backed off and was leaving her alone. In peace. Each decade of my life gets easier, she thought.

Her mind scrolled back to her early years, before she had become a judge. She remembered the women who had come to her for help. Many of them battered. Others the victims of more subtle abuse. They all tried to take it and put on a brave face for as long as they could. Until the day they saw nothing ahead but more and more of the same dreary story. And then they fled.

What was it that brought out the beast in these men, she wondered. What brought this . . . hatred? There was no other word for it, it seemed.

And what made these women make excuses for their husbands' behaviour? It was as if many of them accepted that they were, in some sense, at fault too.

The word *narcissism* came to her mind, taking her back to a lecture she had attended a few months ago. A psychologist had used the word to explain women's persistent belief that they had something to *do* with the way they were being treated. In a sense, they were taking power back in their own hands. Even if it was only an illusion of power. The world is not random, they were saying. It is not one-sided.

Pooja-ben's had not been an arranged marriage. It had been the storybook love marriage. A beautiful, vivacious girl. A tall, handsome, charming man. Her parents had not been happy at all about her choice. But she had been ready to fight to get her way.

The judge thought that Pooja-ben had actually fallen in love with his uniform.

The living room lights of her flat were on. She must have reached already. The maid would have let her in. The judge collected her things and got ready for the trudge up the stairs.

The driver stopped outside her apartment block and handed her his register. She filled in the time and wrote down the number on the kilometre gauge and got out of the car.

The front door was unlocked. The judge stepped inside her flat and her eyes fell on her school friend, her face cleverly but inadequately covered with make-up in an attempt to hide the discoloration of fresh bruises. One eyelid was swollen shut.

'Ami-ben!' she called out. 'I know I'm early. I hope you don't mind!'

The judge sat down heavily. 'I was hoping this was just a small argument. But with you, I should have known better. What happened?'

'He was drunk,' she shrugged. 'And then every little thing I do sets him off.'

'I have seen so much of this that I am actually glad we haven't got rid of prohibition in this state,' the judge sighed.

'There is no such thing as prohibition,' Pooja-ben murmured.

The judge lifted an eyebrow and let it pass.

'Anyway, he had to go out of town this morning. So I thought . . .'

The judge cut her off. 'I'm curious. I want to know what gets into his head when he does things like this. Does he think . . . he is in the lock-up or something?'

Pooja-ben snorted. 'Ami-ben, this is mild milk compared

with what happens in the lock-up.' She paused. 'And it is not as bad as it looks.'

'What do you want me to do?' the judge asked tiredly.

'I . . .'

'Don't you think you have had enough of this nonsense? Isn't it time to get on with your life?'

Pooja-ben hesitated. 'Maybe. But . . .' she looked up at the judge helplessly. 'It is a big step, Ami-ben. I need to think.'

'Well,' the judge offered, 'you can take a break while he is out of town and do your thinking in my guest room. Did you bring clothes to wear tomorrow? Are you all set to stay tonight?'

'Yes.'

'Good. Tomorrow we can go and get any other things you need from home.' She paused, gave her friend a long look. 'Don't be in a rush, Pooja-ben. Don't feel you have to go back home as soon as he sends for you.'

'No . . .'

'You need to get your strength back, so that you can think straight. Right now you are looking so jumpy, so thin. Like a ghost. Maybe it is all that make-up you are wearing.'

Pooja-ben sank into the sofa, tipped her head back against the headrest. 'No,' she said. 'It is not the make-up. I *feel* like a ghost, Ami-ben. I feel hollow. Spent.' She sat up and filled her lungs with air. 'You have no idea how good it is to be out of that house, and far away from *him*.' She looked around at her friend's living room, full of leafy, bushy potted plants all brimming with life. 'All of a sudden I feel as though I can breathe again!'

9

It is true, Adil thought, as he stared wide-eyed at the Shah Alam relief camp the next morning. The old ghosts have left the graveyard. And new ghosts have come!

The Shah Alam relief camp had been set up overnight at the Shah Alam dargah, a shrine built around the grave of the fifteenth-century Sufi saint Hazrat Sayyid Shah Alam. It was a sunny day, and very, very hot, but the courtyard in front of the mosque seemed to be illuminated more with the bands of green and white reflecting off the dargah than the light of day. There were children everywhere, sitting on the platforms around the graves. Women sat in a group on the chabutra, the platform built around the trunk of the 500-year-old banyan tree in front of the mosque, where mothers would tie mannats asking for plentiful breast milk for their infants.

A few older men had installed themselves in the little gatekeeper niche at the entrance to the premises, and had taken on the task of keeping the camp records. They sat busily writing down the names of all the newcomers in their ledgers, and making a note of their injuries.

Vijay had left Adil and Faiza at the camp on his way to

work, so that they could try to trace their mother. He told them he would be back in the evening.

Some of the women sat in the graveyard, to the right of the mosque and the courtyard in front, staring blankly into the distance, not a part of the world of the living. They looked like zombies, Adil thought.

'They won't talk.'

He turned and saw Faiza. She had come back from a round of the graveyard, which extended to the area behind the mosque.

'They are ashamed,' she said. 'They think that what has happened to them is a dishonour to their families.'

'What has happened?'

Faiza hesitated. 'I am only telling you. But this is not for telling anyone else. And not Vijay Uncle. They don't trust the police. They say it is the police only who drove them towards the goondas. Who did everything. So don't tell anyone. You have to promise.'

'Promise.'

'They have been raped by men. Some of them, when they came to the camp, had sticks and iron rods inside them. Still.' She shifted uncomfortably, then turned and discreetly indicated a young woman in the distance who was lying down. 'And they stuck a burning sword inside her.' She hesitated. 'I mean, down below.'

Adil averted his eyes in embarrassment.

'She is going to die, I think. They are afraid to take her to the hospital.'

'But they *have* to take her to the hospital!'

'Bhai, the goondas have been stopping people from going inside the hospital. People who are taking patients. One group . . . The police stopped one group. Asked what religion they were. Then they sent them back here. With burns!'

Adil looked around at the graveyard on their right, shaded by large neem trees. There were people with burns everywhere. Closer to the mosque, some women with burns were sitting on a durrie. A small electric fan had been plugged into an extension board to give them some coolness, some relief.

'And that is not their only problem,' Faiza went on. 'I mean burns. They are not used to so many eyes staring at them all the time. These are the kind of women who have lived all their lives in purdah.'

Adil saw a little girl sitting numbly with her hand resting on a grave.

'They raped her mother. And her aunt. You know what I mean . . . raped? That is when they take off your clothes and then afterwards they burn you. They did this thing in front of her only. Then they cut off their breasts. And then they burnt the two of them until they died. "Don't leave any traces." That was what they said. And she saw everything.'

A little boy sat under a tree with an old man Adil thought must be his grandfather.

'He is the only one in his family who is still alive. He was hiding on the terrace when the rest of the family was trying to run away. He saw when they threw oil and petrol on them and burnt them alive. And diesel. People had come in trucks and were giving it out to the goondas. To burn Muslim people with. Some of the people who burnt them were their neighbours.'

'But his grandfather . . .'

'That is not his grandfather. That is just someone from his locality who has also lost his whole family.' She paused, took a breath. 'He saw them cut open his daughter-in-law's belly and pull out a baby, put it on a trishul, and throw it into the fire . . . Bhai, the goonda who did it, he has done it to *so* many other people. He is still going around. He says they will never put him in jail.'

She paused, looked over her shoulder. 'And they were taking his name too, Bhai. He is a Babu from Bajrangi Dal.'

'Bajrang Dal,' Adil corrected.

'No! They said . . . Well, whatever! But the women were saying . . . And they wouldn't have told *you*. Not about what was done to these women. They saw who was brought in here without clothes, and in what condition. They know how they managed to get away. I was sitting there. And so I listened.'

Adil also needed to get away, to think. He went over to sit with one of the old men who had been writing down names in his ledger. The old man looked up and put down his pen.

'This is not the first time Muslim people are seeing riots in this town,' he said. 'We saw riots during Partition. Then again in '69. In '85. And in '92, after Babri Masjid was broken.' He shook his head. 'But this time is different. This time they are killing women and children as much as men. And they are burning people alive.'

Adil looked up. The sky was still black with smoke. Like the day before.

'This time we cannot go back,' the old man cast his gaze around at the graveyard they had come to. 'This is the end of the world. There is nothing left for us any more. We will never feel safe in this town now.'

Adil went back to sit with Faiza.

'You didn't ... hear anything about Amma, did you, Faizoo?'

'No, Bhai, but I asked. I saw one lady who is a friend of hers. Another teacher. She said she hasn't seen her here, but she will try to find out.'

They both sat in silence on the low wall at the edge of the graveyard and watched the volunteers bring in the supplies to make the lunch. The supplies were all donated to the camp, and some builders near the camp had taken it upon themselves to organize the food.

The lunch was served on large aluminium trays. Adil and Faiza sat with six other children and they ate together from the same tray. Except for one little boy who had to be encouraged to eat, the others tucked into their food calmly. Life must go on.

Faiza went to return the tray so that it could be washed and used again. Already there were thousands of people in the camp to be fed, and more arriving all the time. Meals would have to be handled in shifts.

They were about to head for the shade near the ladies' wazoo-khana, the tank for ablutions before namaaz, when they saw a large woman coming towards them.

'Look, Bhai!' Faiza exclaimed. 'It's my class teacher. Amina Ma'am.'

Adil and Faiza stood up to greet her. She peered at them a moment and then broke into a relieved smile.

'Ae Khuda!' she exclaimed, looking up at the sky. 'A hundred thousand thanks! Nusso-ben's children are safe! We didn't see you anywhere, so we were worried.'

'Where is our mother, Ma'am?' Adil asked formally.

'Son, she is not here. She is in the hospital.'

Adil turned pale, felt his head spin.

'No, son, it is not like that,' her eyes fell on the women with burns lying around the graves. 'I would say she has been lucky.' She paused, searched for the right words. 'She only got hit on the head, and she fell down. Near the school only. Since she was unconscious, they left her alone. Maybe they thought she was dead.'

'But . . .'

'When the goondas left, some of her students found her and took her to hospital. She was still unconscious, last time I heard. But they say she is stable. We will try to take you to see her this evening. If a vehicle is going to V.S. hospital.'

Faiza's legs suddenly buckled under her. She sat down in shock. For the first time since the violence had started Adil saw tears in her eyes.

'So that is why she didn't come . . .'

Amina Ma'am looked helplessly at Adil.

'It's okay, Ma'am,' he said softly. 'I will stay with her.'

Amina Ma'am nodded. 'Take some time,' she said to Faiza. 'Catch yourself. But later on you should come and help me with the children.' She shook her head. 'They are a menace! And the parents need to get away from them now, so that they can get their lives back in order.' And she backed off and returned to her work.

'Don't cry, Faizoo,' Adil said. 'Ma'am said she is stable.'

'I know that, Bhai,' she sobbed. 'But I have to cry now. Because when I go and see her I am not going to cry.'

Adil put his arm around her, said nothing.

'Once . . . once Amma told me about a woman who lived near to them.'

'I know, Faizoo.'

She sniffed. 'All through her life, she had said that when she was going up, dying, she didn't want anyone to cry and call her back. She wanted to go peacefully.' She stopped, stifled a sob. 'Then when she was old and dying, they brought her daughter to see her. And her daughter screamed. And the old lady's eyes rolled before they closed. That was the thing she had always said she didn't want. So I know that if I cry, and she . . .' she broke off, sniffed. 'If I cry, she . . . she won't go peacefully . . .' And then she burst into tears.

Adil felt hot tears fill his eyes too. He squeezed them shut, turned his face away, struggled to regain his composure as the whole world spun out of control. You are the man in the family now, Amma always told him. As long as you are a good boy, everything will be all right.

Would it really? He didn't know any more.

'She will need us to be strong,' he got out at last. 'You are right. But . . . now we will have to be the ones looking after her. Because she is going to get better!'

Faiza opened her eyes. A long faraway look. Then she nodded. 'Yes,' she said firmly. 'Now we know what we have to do.'

She got up and made her way to where a number of small

children sat in a circle. As the afternoon wore on, Adil could see her taking charge of the group, and keeping the children busy. From time to time one of them would look up and say something to her, and she would reply. Crisply. Emphatically. The sound of her lilting voice floated over to where he had been sitting ever since he had heard the news about Amma. And that gave him a sense of assurance that things were going to be all right, after all.

Shortly after the evening namaaz at sunset, Vijay dropped in on his way home from work, as he had promised. He stood at the entrance and scanned the crowd, much larger than it had been in the morning, looking for the two children.

Adil saw him first and went over to greet him.

'Good evening, sir. We have found out about our mother. She is in V.S. Hospital. We hear she is unconscious. But I think there are no other injuries.'

'Come,' Vijay replied brusquely. 'I'll take you there. Where is your sister?'

Adil turned and saw Faiza in a crowd of children, went over and told her to come. She handed over charge, and told Amina Ma'am where she was going.

Then she went with Adil to re-enter the dangerous world outside the graveyard.

10

Adil and Faiza sailed through the streets of Ahmedabad in Vijay's police jeep, crossing on Sardar Bridge to Paldi. The jeep made a U-turn in front of the Kite Museum and approached S.V. hospital through the back roads, entering via the student hostel gate. Vijay's uniform was the best curfew pass, and the best guarantee of safe passage through the crowd in front of the hospital.

A brief halt at the Reception Desk to locate their mother and they proceeded to the ICU, which was just down the corridor.

They found their mother in a bed at the end of the room. The dupatta that always covered her head when she was out of the house was gone. Now there was only a gauze bandage there, on the right side of her head, where she had been hit. A plastic drip bottle hung from a stand next to the bed, with a tube that led to a needle on the back of her hand. She looked as if she was peacefully asleep.

They sat amid the clicks and bleeps of the machines, and waited for the doctors to arrive.

Amma was not the only patient in the ICU who was

unconscious, Adil noted. There was one who seemed to be a road traffic accident victim. Two patients seemed to be recovering from head surgery. There were other patients with problems Adil could not make out. And there were patients who, like Amma, looked as if they had been injured in the mob violence.

Vijay stood up as the doctors entered the room and caught their eye.

'You are relatives?' a young intern came over to inquire.

Vijay pointed to Adil and Faiza. 'She is their mother,' he replied. 'I am a friend of the family.'

Faiza turned and looked up at Vijay with a warm smile.

'We need to fill in her details. Her name is Mrs Nusrat Ansari?'

'Yes,' Adil confirmed. Amma's students had given her name.

'Age?'

Adil hesitated, calculated. 'She is . . . 37 years of age,' he decided.

'Wife of?'

'Our father passed away five years back,' Faiza supplied. 'In this hospital only.'

'Still . . .' the intern showed Adil the form he was filling. Adil nodded and went with him to the table near the door to give the necessary details.

Faiza sat down on a stool next to Amma's bed and looked at her hand, and the needle connected to the drip taped in place. She reached out and touched Amma's other hand, lying palm-up by her side.

Amma's fingers closed around her hand, a gentle squeeze.

Faiza turned in surprise to look at Amma's face, to see if she had woken up. No. Her eyes were still shut, and her face was serene and expressionless.

Adil came back and squatted down next to her.

'Look, Bhai! She is holding my hand!'

'You should talk to her,' a voice behind them said. They turned and saw a slim young Malayali nurse in a white sari looking down at them. 'She is unconscious, but maybe she is hearing what you are saying. So you should talk to her about things she would remember, from the past. It will be good for her.'

Faiza nodded. Vijay was returning with the doctors. They got up and went to hear what they were saying about Amma.

'. . . checked the pupils of her eyes and we don't think there is any major damage. To the brain. Some concussion. And some bruises on her back and legs. Now she is off sedation. We are expecting her to wake up soon. Here . . .' some more papers, 'this is the list of medicines she needs.' The intern looked up at Vijay. 'You have to get them from outside. Sorry, but we don't supply these medicines.'

'No problem,' Vijay said gruffly. He turned and nodded at Faiza and Adil. 'You stay here with her. I will go and get these things.'

They settled down at the bedside, and Faiza took Amma's hand again.

'Bhai? How do we talk to her? She is not going to say anything.'

'Like they talk on the radio?' Adil mused. 'Pretending they are getting replies?'

'Then we should only talk about good things,' Faiza decided. 'Because if she is hearing us she can get upset.' She sat up. 'Amma, remember the time we went to spend holidays with Dadoo? And Dadi? That was the first time we saw the sea. Remember? There was a little boy who lived next to us. Dilnawaz. Remember?'

Adil looked at Amma's face waiting for a reaction. None.

Faiza thought a moment and went on. 'Well, I was thinking we should go back there. For some time.'

A sudden shout in the corridor outside. Men's voices raised. Sounds of a scuffle.

Adil stood up at once, his heart pounding.

Faiza flinched. With an effort of will she turned back to Amma.

'I think they will give us holidays,' she said firmly. 'School is closed these days, you know?'

Jai Shri Ram! Jai Shri Ram! The loud male voices rang out in the corridor. The goons had managed to enter the hospital and were now prowling around as they pleased.

Adil moved away from the bedside and tiptoed to the door to look.

A group of men swaggered past the ICU. Some of them were carrying what looked like crude swords.

'They are drunk!' He heard a contemptuous voice beside him – a woman he had seen in the ward, also come to be with a relative. 'You can smell it from here!'

He slid back into the room and stood in the corner near the door. He turned and looked at Amma, remembered the women he had seen in Shah Alam camp. At least they had removed her dupatta. But still . . .

Then he saw Faiza get up and quietly move the stool around to the other side of Amma's bed. She sat down again, and kept her eyes on the door. The goondas turned and came back. Adil watched them pass the ICU . . . head back towards the reception.

Laughter. Receding.

Suddenly one man burst into the room, a sword in his hand. He started coming down the aisle looking at all the patients. Staring at the family members around the beds. Heading towards Amma.

The sword in his hand caught the light. Glowed.

Like a burning sword!

In horror, Adil watched Faiza slip off her stool. Crouch behind the bed. Waiting.

The man paused, turned his eyes to look at another patient . . .

And Faiza lowered her head like a bull and charged at him. He bellowed as her head hit him right in the pit of his stomach, winded him, sent him sprawling.

A crash. The sound of glass shattering.

The sword flew out of his hand and fell at Faiza's feet.

Adil froze. No!

Quick as a flash, she reached down and grabbed it with both hands.

'Now I am going to kill you!' she shouted. She lifted the sword and pointed it straight at his eyes. '*Tane chhodis nai!*'

Adil watched her circle him. The sword in her hands was as tall as she was. A tiny mongoose stalking a giant cobra.

The man tried to get up, slipped on the wet floor.

Faiza lashed out at him with his sword. He put his arms up to block her. Ducked.

Then Adil saw the long scratch. And the blood.

The man began slithering backwards towards the door.

She raised the sword again.

'Faiza! Stop!'

Vijay. Standing in the doorway.

Adil slumped against the window.

Vijay leaned down and grabbed the goonda and slammed him against the wall. He raised his hand and hit the man, one loud humiliating slap across the face, and then marched him out into the corridor and called for orderlies to remove him from the hospital.

'Faiza,' he said again, gently. 'He's gone. Put that thing down. Now.'

She stood there stiffly. Her eyes glazed.

Adil came and took the sword away from her.

Slowly, the sounds in the room returned. The bleeps and clicks, and the soft whirr of the machines. The voices.

The nurse came and took her hand, led her to a chair. Made her sit down.

Vijay and Adil squatted down beside her.

'He had a sword,' she said. 'If you knew what they did to Muslim women with swords . . .'

'I know, Faiza,' Vijay said.

'You know?'

'Yes.'

She nodded, not taking her eyes off the sword, now on the floor.

'Come,' said Vijay. 'Let's go home. I think you need a break.'

She shook her head. 'No. Now I will stay here. With her.' She looked up at Vijay. 'When he was down on the floor and I was the one with the sword, I saw in his eyes that he was a coward.' She wrinkled her nose, shifted her glasses higher. 'Now I am not afraid. I know I can look after her.'

'Let her stay tonight,' the nurse suggested.

Vijay looked around the room. All the other patients in the ward had a relative who was planning to stay the night. It was only their patient who was unattended.

'Fair enough.' He agreed. 'I'll post one of my men in the corridor to see that this kind of thing doesn't happen again. Be good, Faiza. Don't kill anybody tonight. I'll see you tomorrow morning.' He turned. 'Adil?'

'I will stay with her, sir.'

They watched him leave. Then Faiza bent down and picked up the sword, brought it back with her and stood it up carefully next to Amma's bed.

Then she sat down on the little stool, as though nothing had happened. Took Amma's hand again, and resumed their conversation.

11

'I decided to take a look at some of the material I had on Ahmedabad. Since you are going there again. To refresh my memory too.' Shama handed me a book, carefully wrapped in old newspaper. 'It's all here. Our report. What our medical team saw when we went to the camps.'

I took it and skipped past the introduction.

'What I like in this book are the anecdotes,' she continued. 'More than the report. They give you a real feel of the women themselves. And what they went through. I think only one of these cases found its way into an FIR. They knew there was no point going to the police. And there was no way we could get these women to speak out.' Shama shook her head. 'So in a way, all this has vanished. For the official record, it never happened.'

The rumours had not vanished though. I had heard her talk of the particular violence that had been unleashed on Muslim women and children in Gujarat in the 2002 violence. But seeing it down in black-and-white was overwhelming.

Shama caught my expression. 'Even I felt like that when I opened the book. I got . . . upset, all over again.'

In my mind's eye I suddenly saw a parade of images, all the people I had seen during my visits to Ahmedabad. A few real heroes who towered above the crowd, like neem trees, giving shade to many and keeping mosquitoes away. And nervous vines, meaning well but suddenly afraid to climb the tall trees, preferring to lie low in the underbrush. And then there were the 'nice' Hindus, old family friends emboldened by the suddenly changed environment, the ones who smilingly dismissed the violence as a small matter. And others that I had only seen on the street, whose expressions I would keep trying to read. Could people like these, sane, *courteous* people, have condoned this sort of thing? Or even joined in something as atavistic as this?

'I'm still trying to get a sense of how this happened,' I said.

'Arrey, you *know*!'

'No,' I insisted. 'I mean: how do you get normal average people to feel okay about something like this?'

'This has been going on for a long time,' Shama began.

'Beware of normal people, Deepa Auntie!' a voice broke in from the corner of the room.

I turned: Shama's daughter, an art student, was sitting cross-legged on the floor with a sketchpad in front of her, completing a drawing of a broken flowerpot.

'"Good" people!' she growled. 'They are the *baddest* people in the world!'

'Arrey, what are you saying, Nida?'

'You know the kind of people I mean: the ones who happily send off their sons to die on the battlefield. Who *understand* why you should kill your neighbours. The ones who *know* that you should always follow the stream.' She frowned. 'And they even think the best artist is a *dead* artist!'

'Haanh. She's right. Deepa, long before people were able to see themselves as individuals they were simply part of a group. There was no such thing, until recent times, as people having separate identities. Or a personal conscience. So these modern-day people, the ones she is calling "good", are only following an old, old programming.'

'Give me *baaaad* people any day! At least they can think for themselves!' And she picked up her pencil and sketchpad and stalked off to her room.

'It's one thing to *understand* about killing neighbours,' I persisted. 'But to *do* it?'

'Deepa, I don't know if I told you about the time they invited us to come and talk to them.'

'Who?'

'Groups,' she said cryptically.

'What groups?'

'Groups that had been active in the riots.' She broke off. Shook her head. 'I felt my hair standing on end at the thought, you know? How you would feel if they told you to walk through a snake pit? I was about to say no. But then one of the women said: "We have no problems with Muslims like *you*."' She paused for effect.

I was taken by surprise. What had they meant by that? No problems with Muslims from Delhi? No problems with educated Muslims? Muslim lady doctors? Shias?

'So I went,' Shama continued. 'I was curious. I thought I should. To get our point of view across. And we talked to them. They were polite, they listened.' She smiled ruefully. 'But in the end, it was no use. They had made up their minds. What they said was, "Well, this time it was necessary."'

Necessary . . . I shuddered, coming back to my original question. 'But I wasn't thinking about the hardcore fundamentalists. I was wondering about how ordinary everyday people, the kind who are too lazy, or too scared to get into things like this, suddenly change. Turn rogue.'

'They have been working at this for a long time,' Shama went back to her earlier argument too. 'Working with kids. Teaching them to hate. Have you ever been to one of their schools? For poor children?'

'I haven't been, but I've heard about them. Shishu Mandirs.'

'Yes. Of course, the parents are very happy: their children are being given an education. Education free of cost for the underprivileged, that's what they call it. And in a local language they can understand. But it comes with a lot of brainwashing. Motivational stories, they call them. Stories that build pride in a Hindu past by teaching the children to hate Muslims. They start each day with a solid dose of this. Songs and prayers and rituals. Just imagine the sense of belonging, and how exciting it must feel to a little child!'

A parade of images scrolled through my mind. Of goons on the street with crude weapons, and jerry cans of petrol and diesel. All this . . . from education?

'I can see this sort of schooling setting the groundwork for communal violence, but just the groundwork. There is something more that I am not able to wrap my brain around. What I mean is: it isn't so easy to translate all this *information* the kids are getting in school into action. People don't just get up and do horrendous things because they hear that they are supposed to.'

'It makes a difference if they are children. And impressionable.'

'Yes. I agree. But still ... I think it has to be something more complex than this. People can *justify* all this to themselves later by talking about the past. But getting up and *doing* it is a different matter. No, there is something missing.'

'Arrey, what world are you living in, Deepa? You should hear the kinds of things the police say there: that all Muslim boys are sure to be guilty of *something*, that all they ever talk about is crime. Just imagine what a man like that is thinking when he gets his hands on a Muslim boy in the lock-up. You *know* what happens to them.'

'I have an idea,' I said softly. 'But it must be worse than I imagine.'

'And *why* do some of them turn to crime?' Shama went on. 'Can they even get jobs when they apply?'

I remembered a Diwali party I had gone to in Mumbai. At a friend's home. They were playing cards for high stakes, and the topic of Muslims came up. One man boasted that, in his company, he never allowed employees leave on Muslim holidays. Another guest one-upped him by saying that he only employed them as labour, never in management. And the third said that he never employed them at all.

I squirmed under her gaze. 'I guess what I meant was that I was wondering how this kind of self-indulgent talk gets transformed into mob violence. It feels more like a background drone than something setting up to erupt . . .'

'But you saw, Deepa. It did erupt. Where did that come from?'

'I know,' I frowned. 'But ... how do I put it? Hate is not the emotion that comes to mind when I look at how things stand between Hindus and Muslims in Ahmedabad. Now. There must have been strong emotions a few years back, during the violence. There must have been. But it looks almost as though they have dwindled down to ... indifference. To resignation.' I paused again, groping for the right words. 'It's as if both Hindus and Muslims now live in two separate universes. Two opposite sides of the river. When I talk to Hindus I get the sense that they don't actually *know* the Muslim community ...'

'I don't think they ever did.'

'Yes. It's as though Muslims are something to look at under a microscope. Something ... strange, alien. And that's when these people are trying to be nice! It's almost like the way they talk about the Moors in Spain, or the Incas, or the Aztecs. Like people they need to ... speculate about, because they aren't there anymore ...'

'They were only being nice because they were talking to you,' Shama sniffed, and got up and headed for the kitchen to make us some chai. I followed her, carrying the khakra and chhundo, the paper-thin crisp flatbread and sweet mango pickle that I had brought her from Ahmedabad, and reached up for a plate. There, I stood and stared at the water swirling around in the little saucepan as it came to a boil.

Something about the emergence of structure ...

'What?'

'It's just that I've never ever seen little people get up one by one and decide to take things to the next level. That isn't how things happen.' I hesitated, then decided to forge ahead. 'Like with languages. You never see dialects coming together and making a new language just because they *can*. No. It's always an *event* that sets it all in motion. Something external. New rulers. Changes in the economy. A disaster. Then this gets reflected in how the dialects behave . . .'

'But we are talking about people, Deepa. Not languages.'

I shook my head. 'It's all the same,' I insisted. 'The same laws of nature. How individual elements behave when circumstances change . . .' I broke off. *Was* it all the same?

Shama poured the water into a teapot, added tea leaves and gave it a stir, put the tea cosy on top. Found six mugs and carried it all on a tray to the living room. I followed her with the khakra and chhundo. Then she poured out three mugs of tea, added lots of milk and sugar, and took them to Nida's room, which was in the process of being painted in bright yellows and greens.

The two painters took their mugs of tea, and she gave the third to a little boy with an intense, inscrutable expression. She also put a plate of biscuits on the ladder for him.

No, I suddenly decided. It was never the little people who remade the world. Like those nouns and verbs that spoke of brighter days, the most they could do was simply disappear off a bad scene. Leaving the language, and the world it had lived in, duller and less colourful.

'There is more to Gujarat than just Ahmedabad,' Shama said, as she lifted the tea cosy again and started to pour for us.

'These people . . .' she inclined her head and pointed to the painters, 'have come from a different Gujarat. The sort of long-ago place that I didn't think existed anymore.'

'Where?'

'It's near the coast. A little Muslim mohalla in Surat. Next time, I'm going to give Ahmedabad a miss and head straight there.'

12

'There is a man here to see you,' the nurse whispered to Adil.
'He is outside the ICU. He says he is your uncle.'

Uncle? Adil frowned, straightened the dupatta over his
mother's head and got up to investigate.

A tall figure stood in the doorway. 'Salaam w'aleikum,
Adil. I came as soon as I heard. The last few days it wasn't
safe to travel. It still is not too safe, but . . .'

Adil quickly reconnected with the larger world beyond
Ahmedabad. His father's brother had heard the news and
come. 'Chacha! W'aleikum salaam!' He gave his uncle a hug.
'But how did you come to know about Amma?'

'Son, we were worried about the three of you. The news
from this place was very bad. We had been trying to contact
you. And then your sister wrote to your Dada and told him
how your mother had been injured, and that she was in this
hospital. In the ICU. And she asked if the three of you could
stay with us. So he sent me. We thought that since your
mother cannot teach now . . .'

'Faiza wrote to you?'

'Yes. How is your mother?'

'She is a bit better. She was unconscious for some days. And then one day, when the nurse was turning her over, she opened her eyes. And now she has started talking, but she doesn't remember anything about what happened to her. That whole day is missing from her mind. She doesn't know anything about the riots.'

'That may be a blessing.' His uncle paused. 'She will be able to travel?'

'I don't know. I have to ask the doctors. But how would we go?'

'Bus is safest, I think,' his uncle replied. 'Not train. Not yet.'

Adil's heart sank. A bus ride! Amma would certainly not be able to sit up for the whole journey.

'Is she awake?' his uncle asked.

'She should wake up soon.' He looked into the room. The nurse had screened off Amma's bed. 'Come, Chacha, we can sit outside for some time. I think the nurse is attending to her.'

The waiting area next to the ICU was a patio, open to the sky. Adil and his uncle walked past and went out the front entrance. They got two cups of tea from the chaiwala outside the hospital and came back and found a bench.

They sat together in the clear morning light and sipped their tea.

'Son, you don't have to worry about paying for this,' his uncle said, putting down his empty cup. 'Between me and your Dada, we will manage. But the faster we finish with this place . . .'

'The hospital is free, Chacha. We only have to pay for her medicines. Things like that.'

His uncle frowned. 'You have been paying? You were able to take out money from the bank for this?'

'N-no,' Adil stammered. 'A friend has helped us.'

'A friend?'

'A p-police officer. He rescued me and Faiza the first night, Chacha. He took us to his home, and then he helped us to find Amma.' He paused, centred himself. 'I don't think we would even have been able to reach this hospital without him. The roads were too dangerous. They were stopping Muslim people, and sending everyone back to the relief camps.'

'We have been hearing a different story about the police in Ahmedabad.'

'I know. I heard him talking one night. He thought I was asleep. How they are not allowed to stop the riots.' He remembered the mouse that had stopped to stare at him on the floor. 'And it is true: many of them are no different from the goondas.'

'Why is he helping you?'

'I don't know. He doesn't have children. And he thinks we are from a good family. I heard him saying that.' Conscience, he remembered suddenly. 'And he doesn't agree with the government.'

'Will he help us to find a way to take your mother back with us?'

'He may be the best person to ask.'

That evening when Vijay came to the hospital, they sat together in the waiting area to make plans.

'Definitely not by train,' Vijay decided. 'And not by bus either. The situation has eased up a bit, but not enough for you to take chances. This morning we were allowed to move against the rioters and stop some of the looting that is going on. But this thing will not end so fast. It is a mess.' He thought a moment. 'You need a vehicle which is not going to take on passengers along the way. You don't want strangers looking at her . . .' he pointed his chin towards the ICU, 'and asking questions.'

'You mean we have to go by car?' Faiza asked.

'No. If they stop your car, *you* might be able to manage. And Adil.' He turned to their uncle. 'But you cannot pass off as a Hindu. Not a chance.' He shook his head. 'And their mother can't either. No, I am thinking of something else. Give me a few days to set it up.'

Three days later, at noon, they went with Vijay to a warehouse on the outskirts of Ahmedabad. There, a colourful old truck, bound for Mumbai via Surat, was being loaded with sacks of onions. The driver helped them put a cotton mattress on the floor of the tray for Amma so that she could lie down out of sight. Faiza and their uncle would ride in the back with her. Adil would sit with the driver and the loader in front.

'I'll see you when you come back next month for your Boards, Adil. Study hard!'

'I will, sir. Thank you for everything.'

They walked with Faiza to the back and helped her climb into place. Then the back of the tray was lifted and bolted shut.

Faiza climbed up and stuck her head out from under the tarpaulin. She took a last look at Vijay and lifted her hand in a wistful little wave.

'Bye, Uncle,' she said softly.

'Look after yourself, Faiza,' he replied.

Adil took his place in front and the driver started the engine.

The truck stumbled out of the warehouse and headed for a petrol pump to fill diesel. Then they made for the highway and turned south towards Surat.

The NH8 was called an intercity highway, but it didn't feel as though they had left the city behind. There was hardly any sense of being in the countryside: on both sides of the road, the shops went on and on.

'Looking like less traffic today,' the driver broke in on Adil's thoughts. 'But picking up. Has to start again. If trucks do not ply, the whole world will come to a stop.'

Adil nodded. He looked out the window. Interspersed with the shops were the blackened remnants of buildings that had been burnt to the ground. The shops next to them, however, had been totally spared.

'They came all the way here. Burnt down those shops,' the driver explained. 'On the highway! All the way to Bharuch. After that, nothing.'

'Nothing?'

'End of riots. Bharuch, Surat, both are clear. Well, a little bit of violence the first day, but after that nothing.' He drove a few minutes in silence. 'So I am not stopping this truck till Bharuch.' A pause. 'Anyhow, no reason to stop. No dhabas.'

Adil scanned the line of shops for a few minutes. It was true. He didn't see any roadside eateries where they could have stopped for a quick meal.

'Goondas knew who was who, you see,' the driver went on. 'Had lists. Look over there.' He pointed. 'Used to be a vegetarian dhaba. Nice place. Cheap.'

Adil suddenly knew what was coming next.

'Owner was a Muslim.' The driver nodded grimly. 'These things they knew.'

Adil felt his mood beginning to unravel. 'What if they stop us?'

The driver shrugged. 'Won't happen. Not interested in trucks. And I am driving the same speed as the other trucks. Not standing out.' He turned, looked at Adil. 'If you see crowds anytime, dikra, don't look. Because they will look back. Better to look bored. Like him ...' He pointed to the loader sitting in the window seat lost in his own thoughts.

The loader came to life and grinned shyly. 'Boss, nobody ever stopped this truck. Up to now. So relax!'

They made it past Baroda without incident, and Adil felt his nerves beginning to settle. The signs of violence had also begun to reduce. He hoped his mother was sleeping through this.

Just after Bharuch, they stopped at a roadside tea stall, and Adil went out and got cups of tea for all of them. The driver and the loader stayed in their seats in front, dipping bhakris into their tea, while Adil climbed into the back of the truck and sat with the rest of his family.

They brought out the theplas that Vijay's wife had sent them for the journey, and ate a late lunch.

Amma was awake, and sat cradling her teacup in her hands.

'I am beginning to think this is not a dream,' she said at last. 'This is real.'

'Yes,' Adil said softly. 'It is real. But don't worry. We'll be reaching Surat in, maybe, two hours.'

Amma's eyes suddenly misted. 'I'm sorry you have to do this for me.'

'Amma!' Faiza retorted. 'I was the one who decided we should make this long trip. So *you* don't have to be sorry.' She shrugged. 'And I am not sorry at all!'

Amma blinked, tried to remember. Looked up at Adil at last. 'Your Boards? They were to be ... about now! You should be there!'

'No, Amma. They were postponed. Now they are going to be next month. I'll go back for them.' He took her empty cup. 'You and Faiza will come later. Next term. Schools are closed these days, in any case.'

'And by next term, you will be better,' Faiza decided.

'Yes ...' Her voice trailed off, and she drifted back to sleep.

A rap on the side of the tray told Adil it was time to go. He climbed down, returned the cups, and got back in front with the driver for the last lap of the journey.

The driver put the truck in first gear and tuned in to Radio Mirchi. As they began to move, an upbeat song faded on, and kept pace with them as they changed gears. Adil saw in his mind's eye a different vehicle, a little sports car, and a different road.

When they were in high gear and running at highway

speed, the words came on. Three friends, all of them young and brimming over with hope, were on a road trip. Adil turned and looked at the driver and the loader.

Dil chahta hai, went the words.

Yes, Adil thought. Let us hope.

The driver smiled when he saw Adil's buoyant mood and turned up the volume.

What a strange journey this is, the song went. None of us knows where he is going, and what the future holds.

But still . . .

Dil chahta hai . . .

Adil followed the music into the film and entered another landscape. He was walking along a beach, somewhere far, far away. And walking beside him was a girl with almond eyes the colour of golden-green pistachios, her face framed by a peach-coloured dupatta.

He allowed himself to drift with the dream.

It was getting towards evening when they crossed the Tapi river. They got down and waited for a bus for the last part of their journey. The air had turned cool, with a tang that spoke of the sea.

The sun began to set in a blaze of glory.

Yes, Adil thought, a day of fire is coming to an end. Many days of fire. Those were not a dream. But the days after today will be a dream, for as long as we are here. We will be able to shut our eyes and forget. For a time.

He turned and looked at his mother, standing with Faiza, looking almost like her old self. And as the pink glow of the sunset lit up her face, he wondered if everything was suddenly going to be all right.

13

'The Railway Ministry has come out with its own report about the Godhra fire,' Ramya said, putting down the stapled booklet in her hand. 'This report came out about a year ago. Their technical team came to a totally different conclusion about the cause of the fire in Coach S6.'

We were high in the air on a flight to Ahmedabad. My second court appearance, the cross examination, was scheduled for the following morning.

'I heard about it. Wanted to read it. Is that a copy?'

She nodded. 'It makes sense. A pity it won't be entered as evidence in the court in Ahmedabad. The Godhra trial is a State subject. Unless they specifically request this report, they don't need to look at it, or at any a document from the Central Government.'

The Godhra Trial. Fifty-eight Muslim men had been jailed as terrorists for conspiracy to set fire to the train, and were still awaiting trial. An elaborate conspiracy, absurdly large, involving all these men getting together and buying and hoarding drums of fuel. And waiting for a train running more than five hours late, to set alight a coach full of kar sevaks, none of whom had tickets or reservations, such that they could have been said to be expected.

I remembered the gist of the Railway Report, but I didn't know the details. The gist was that the fire was accidental, and essentially identical to another fire that had happened in an unoccupied bogie that was in the railway yard waiting to be cleaned, a case where no arson had been suspected.

I took the report from Ramya and leafed through until I came to the section titled 'The Fire'.

Thermodynamics, to an engineer, is a physical science that dates back to the first steam engines that were used to pull passenger trains. To an engineer, thermodynamics is the study of heat and radiation and its interaction with materials within a closed system. But to a linguist, it is a metaphor that allows insights into the behaviour of almost all the quasi-living systems we find interesting. Languages. Communities. The Market. The sun itself, I often thought.

I myself often used the metaphor of non-equilibrium thermodynamics to explain the birth of new hybrid languages within a single generation. Or the behaviour of human groups. It was a useful way of understanding how individual elements could join forces and become a structured mass, which would operate according to different rules, new rules that would characterize an emergent living system. An entity existing far-from-equilibrium, feeding from an energy source without which it would collapse and return to its base state.

Like a modern global city, supremely networked and connected to a dedicated power grid, which could find itself suddenly plunged into darkness and chaos if its plug were pulled.

The most flammable material in the coach, I read, was the latex foam that filled the seats: the seat covers themselves were flame-resistant. The second most flammable material was the plywood under this foam, the base of the seats. Luggage stored below the seats could have caught fire from anything burning – a cigarette butt, a matchstick – and smouldered unnoticed for a good long while until it finally ignited the plywood.

Once the plywood had ignited, it would have set the latex foam on fire, and this would release enormous clouds of hot, dense, asphyxiating, black smoke. This smoke itself would become the source of ignition for other materials as the temperature rose to flash point. At this stage, the initially flame-resistant rexine seat covers would melt and vaporize, along with the laminated plastic partitions and the linoleum flooring. These materials would then also produce hot dense toxic smoke containing hydrogen cyanide, isocyanates and carbon monoxide.

The dense high temperature smoke would have spread to the top of the carriage and moved along the ceiling, and in the space between the ceiling and the roof, throughout the length of the coach. The radiative and convective heat that it generated would eventually have resulted in a 'flash over', when fire would engulf the entire coach from the top downwards.

That would explain why the burn injuries on the survivors were always on their heads or shoulders, never lower down. There had been no fire on the floor while the survivors were leaving the carriage. The heat then had been radiating down from above.

The people who had gotten burnt in the coach had not been able to leave because they had been unconscious. Because of the toxic smoke.

Flash over.

I read these words again and the penny dropped. That was the moment when the hot smoke took on a life of its own, metamorphosed into a raging fire. No longer a collection of inert individual substances at ground state – plywood, foam, rexine, sunmica and linoleum – but a force. Something that could kill.

Like seawater energized by an earthquake to become a tsunami.

No wonder I had been so unconvinced by what Shama had said: that the whole state of Gujarat had been indoctrinated from childhood, taught to hate Muslims, and that this by itself had caused the carnage. As a teacher, I knew how difficult it was to get students excited about anything, how dispiriting it was to get people to believe so strongly in a cause that they were willing to go out on the streets, even for a peace march.

No, there had to be something more. Something that could transform ordinary fence-sitters into active sympathizers, and sympathizers into vicious brutes ready to participate in a carnage. There had to be an injection of heat energy to bring the phase change that would erase individual consciences and create a killer mob.

There had to be a flash over.

The materials had to be, to some extent, flammable. And there needed to be a spark, then a period of smoulder. And an initial combustion that would bring the temperature up to flashpoint.

And create a single high-energy entity.

Something organically linked and moving as one.

I turned to Ramya. 'Why wasn't this report picked up? By anyone? I can imagine the Gujarat government not being overjoyed about it, but what about all the others? Lawyers, activists . . .'

She shrugged. 'I think they are not ready to believe that the whole Godhra thing could have been unprovoked. They have invested too much in the idea that Muslims *did* start the fire, but that the riots were out of proportion to the provocation.' She paused. 'And they have their own reports. One of their investigators said he talked to Muslims in Godhra, and they confidentially told him that they did slip little burning wicks in the window slats to "smoke out" the goondas who they thought had abducted a Muslim woman and taken her into S6. That they set the fire, but unintentionally.'

'What about *you*?'

She looked out the window at a passing cloud. 'But I *did* help with the Railway Ministry report. I helped them when they were doing the investigation.'

'You could have used the findings. In court. Why didn't you?'

She let the moment pass. Then, apropos of nothing, she went on. 'If you don't look at something for long enough, it tends to vanish. Then if someone picks it up and tries to talk about it, they say she is just a crank, always bringing up non-issues.'

'Like my doctorate,' I put in dryly. 'Everyone refuses to recognize it, refuses to address it, and so it vanishes. Then I look like a crank when I want to be called "Dr". So they put on their best patronizing expressions and do it just once. Just to humour me. Then they make it vanish again.' I nodded. 'Tell me about it!'

'Your fault, Deepi. You're supposed to keep it in focus.'

'Yeah.' A thought struck me. 'Ramya? Did I tell you about the time my house nearly burnt down?'

'It did?'

I nodded. 'I had gone to sleep one night after guests had left. Someone must have dropped a cigarette butt on a mattress on the floor of my living room. A mattress stuffed with cotton. I woke up two hours later coughing. And I went to turn off the cooler. I thought it must be pulling in smoke from leaves burning outside.'

She looked at me more intently now.

'And then I saw that the fire was *inside* my living room. It had taken two whole hours for the mattress to smoulder and burst into flames. They were leaping at least a metre high. Right next to a plywood cabinet!'

'How did you put it out?'

'I rigged up a hose from the kitchen sink and flooded the mattress with water. And then I dragged it out of the house. And went back to sleep. But then I got a call from my neighbour a few hours later. The mattress had burst into flames again in the driveway!'

It was still smouldering deep inside.

That the violence in Gujarat had been carefully nurtured

and stage-managed by parties with a vested interest had always been a certainty. The only mystery had been the behaviour of the general population. Now it all made a kind of sense: all the giggles, the jokes about Muslims during the violence from educated people who, one expected, would have been more sensitive. The absolute bestiality of the mobs. The strange belief of many bystanders that they had, in some sense, been a part of the movement. That they had been active.

It was as though every human being in the mob had jumped one level up, to orbit the nucleus at the next-higher level of energy.

Even if someone *had* burnt the carriage, it didn't justify the carnage that was unleashed upon the Muslims of Gujarat afterwards. But now I was convinced that *no one* had burnt that carriage. I was certain that the fire under the seat must have been in gestation for a good while before the clash on the Godhra platform took place.

An accidental fire had been used to create a deliberate flash over.

I thought of all the shamans before me who had stared into the flames and seen the light.

14

Sunrise.

Adil closed his chemistry book and turned off the lamp next to his pillow, got up and folded his bedding and put it away. Looked around the living room to make sure it bore no signs of its night-time role as his bedroom.

His grandmother was already in the kitchen making chai for everyone. She looked up and gave him a warm smile.

He took his chai and went back to sit in the living room.

There was the sound of bare feet on the floor. Faiza came in and settled herself on the divan across the room with her chai, tucking her feet up under her.

'Amma wants to go shopping today,' she lilted. 'You want to come?'

He shook his head. 'I told Dilnawaz I was going to take him for a last look at the sea with me before I left.'

'Anything you need to take back with you tomorrow?'

'Nothing special. If you think of anything, just get it.'

She wagged her head. 'Amma says better take some food. To last a few days. You don't know what it will be like there.' She frowned. Switched gears abruptly. 'How will you go? I mean today?'

'On cycles. Uncle says I can take his.'

'Well, don't go too fast. Dilnawaz is still small.'

After breakfast Adil headed next door. Dilnawaz was waiting for him outside.

'Baba says even we might go, Adil-bhai. Just like you,' he said solemnly.

'To Ahmedabad?'

'No-no. Baba wants us to go from Gujarat.'

'Where? Bombay?'

Dilnawaz shook his head unsmilingly. 'No. We will go to Delhi. My Chacha is already there. We can stay with him for some time. Then we will get our own house.'

Adil followed Dilnawaz into his house. His nostrils twitched at the smell of all the different paints and solvents his friend's father had. Like a chemistry lab, he thought.

Adil greeted the father. 'Salaam w'aleikum, Uncle. Dilnawaz says you are planning to shift!'

'Adil!' he replied heartily. 'So he has told you?'

'Yes. To Delhi?'

'Thinking. Just thinking. My younger brother is there, and he had the idea that we should go too. It is a good idea.' He shook his head sadly. 'Gujarat is not the place for us now.'

'But Surat is safe!'

'Yes, but for how long? It is not beyond this government to start a problem where none exists. I prefer to be careful, and not trust too much.'

'When will you leave?'

'Not fixed yet. I will see how it goes. What about you?'

Adil frowned. 'I have to do my Boards.'

'Yes, Boards.' Dilnawaz's father stared out the window a while. 'And then?'

Adil paused. 'I wasn't thinking about after that, Uncle.'

'Well, Adil. My feeling is that you should take some time and think. Soon. About shifting.' The older man shrugged. 'I know it is not easy to pull up roots and start over again. But sometimes it is the only way.'

'Start over again!'

'For us it is not so difficult as it sounds. Everywhere there is work for a good painter. We will manage.' He smiled. 'So finish your Boards. By then we will know for sure. And if we go, you have a place in Delhi. Any time.'

Adil cycled off with Dilnawaz towards Dumas Beach, suddenly seeing everything around him with new eyes. A last look. The end of a dream, he remembered. Tomorrow would be a return to reality.

As he caught sight of the sea, he turned and saw Dilnawaz cycling urgently behind him on his little bicycle, looking as intent as ever. He slowed down and started to coast, waited for the boy to come up alongside.

'Look, Adil-bhai,' he gasped, catching his breath and lifting one hand to point. 'Picture ni shooting chale chhe!'

Adil looked the length of the beach and saw a video camera mounted on a tripod under a palm tree. A large bear of a man was looking through the viewfinder.

'Wow!' Adil burst out. 'Shooting! I want to see this!'

They parked their cycles and walked down to the beach. The cameraman looked up and saw them coming, his bored expression clearing to a ghost of a smile. He cocked his head at Adil and finally lifted an eyebrow. Come . . .

'Is it . . . can I stay and watch?' Adil asked hopefully.

'Why not?' the cameraman mused. 'We have not started yet. The kids have gone for a recce.'

'Kids?'

'Students,' the cameraman clarified. 'This is a student production. They wanted a few beach shots from here.' He turned and stared into the distance. Some long-haired young men in bright clothes were headed their way. 'They are coming back. Let us go.'

He shouldered the camera, picked up the tripod with his other hand and motioned to Adil and Dilnawaz to follow him with the reflectors.

'Break mari gyu!' Dilnawaz breathed. 'This is our big break, Adil-bhai!'

'Sohail-bhai!' One of the students pointed to a spot and turned to face the water, making a frame with his fingers. 'Here.'

The cameraman handed the camera to Adil and got busy setting up the tripod. Adil casually hefted the camera onto his shoulder and stole a glance through the lens.

The day proceeded in shots, like a dream sequence, with the sea murmuring in the background. At noon, the cameraman pointed at the sun and called for a break.

'Top light,' he announced.

Adil and Dilnawaz sat with him as they waited for the students to come back with their lunch.

'By the way, my name is Sohail,' he said.

'And I am Adil,' Adil replied shyly. 'What is this film?'

'I am not sure. It is not part of their coursework. It looks like a corporate video. They will be taking the rest of the shots in Ahmedabad.'

'Oh? I'm going back to Ahmedabad tomorrow!'

'You are from Ahmedabad?' Sohail raised an eyebrow. 'Where?'

'Jamalpur.'

'Ah! Well I live in Paldi. Just across the river from you!'

Adil felt a question form inside his head. He looked up at Sohail.

'Yes?' Sohail prompted.

'I . . . I was wondering how you . . . got into this line. I mean, how you got to be a cameraman.'

'Oh! It was my father's idea.' He looked out at the sea. 'I had finished school, and I could not get a job. None of my friends was getting a job. So we just hung out together. A gang. Time-pass.' He smiled. 'Well, my father started to worry. Said there were only two places a Muslim boy was likely to end up. One was jail . . .'

'Jail! But why?'

'He said it was only a matter of time before we did something that would be of interest to the police. We knew enough other boys who were getting into that kind of thing.'

'Jail and . . .?'

'The film industry. The only other place where someone like me would stand a chance. He knew a man in Bombay who made documentaries. He asked him to take me in hand.' Sohail paused. 'He was a good man. He did not need me: he himself was a cameraman. But he still took me. And now . . .' he shrugged.

'Come,' one of the students called out. 'Let's eat.'

Adil's dream sequence continued into the afternoon. He held up a reflector as Sohail shouldered the camera and walked along the beach, keeping one of the students in the frame.

Cut.

Sohail played back the shot to check for camera jerks. None. Smooth as silk. He smiled to himself.

All too soon, they were lining up the last shot. A fishing boat crossing the horizon with a fringe of palm leaves at the top of the frame.

'It keeps the sun out of the frame,' Sohail explained softly to Adil, as he cupped his large paw over the top of the lens to shade it. 'The camera cannot handle that.'

'Roll . . .'

Adil felt himself gliding with the boat and sailing into the sunset. A sound track was fading on inside his head. He recognized the song.

'Cut.'

Adil started, felt himself jerked back abruptly into a large over-bright world.

'Is it a pack up?' He heard Sohail's low growl.

'Just a minute.'

One of the students pulled out a piece of paper and crossed off something with a ballpoint pen. 'I think so . . . Yes . . . Yes! Pack up!'

Sohail lifted the camera off the tripod, and Adil and Dilnawaz ran and picked up the reflectors to take them to the car and pack them for the ride back to Ahmedabad.

Adil stood back from the door, held his breath. Let this moment never end . . .

Right on cue, Sohail turned and gave him a long look. He dipped his hand into a pocket and fished out his visiting card.

'Take my card,' he said, handing it to Adil. 'And call me when you get back to Ahmedabad.'

'Of . . . of course!'

'Maybe there will be some work for a camera assistant.'

'That would be great!' he breathed.

The car started and the group drove off.

The two boys cycled back to Surat in the shadowless light of a perfect evening. Adil turned to look at Dilnawaz pedalling alongside him. The boy's eyes were full of starry dreams.

Then Adil heard the soundtrack fade on again inside his head. He was walking on a beach, a video camera perched on his shoulder. In the viewfinder was a tight shot of a pair of feet walking away from him on the sand. He gently zoomed out and tilted up to a full shot. A peach-coloured dupatta came into the frame and the girl turned, looked at him with eyes as golden bright as the afternoon sun.

Dil chahta hai . . .

The girl inside the frame turned and resumed her walk, and Adil followed, keeping the shot as smooth as silk. And then they were home again. Cut.

'Adil-bhai! We will do this again,' Dilnawaz declared. 'One day. You and I will shoot a film together in Delhi, Inshallah.' He paused. 'I will write to you.'

Amma was sitting up in the living room with Dadi, her cheeks glowing from her day's outing with Faiza. Like old times, Adil thought. The bad days are behind us.

'Dadi is making payas for you,' Faiza announced. 'She says they will be ready by breakfast tomorrow. And you can take some back with you.'

Adil followed his grandmother into the kitchen and sniffed the heavenly aroma of the mutton shanks she knew he loved.

He paused and mentally framed the last shot of the dream: his grandmother's smile.

15

I looked up from my breakfast of fafda and green papaya chutney and saw a large shape looming over our table and blocking all the light. Jaafer-bhai. He slid onto the bench next to me and gave Ramya a charming smile.

'Sorry, Madam, for late.'

She fixed him with a cold stare.

'But I have eaten and come, Madam. Not to worry.'

She considered him silently for a few moments. Then she turned abruptly to Anoop, sitting next to her with a cup of masala chai in front of him, and started the briefing. 'I want the three of you to keep the discussion focused on the confessions. The prosecution is going to try to discredit you as witnesses. Don't get distracted.'

'Wait!' I protested. 'This is a cross-examination! Don't we have to take our cue from the kind of questions we get?'

'I'm not saying that you don't answer them,' she cut in calmly. 'But you have to frame your answers carefully. I want the judge to stay tuned to the analysis of the confessions.'

'I don't know,' I frowned. 'I thought I was meant to be an expert witness. You know, just available to answer questions.

If I try to push the discussion only in the direction I want, I might lose my credibility. With the judge. I'm supposed to *look* unbiased.'

'No!' she countered sharply. 'You're only supposed to make sure we win.' She held my gaze, willing me to burn that word into my mind. Win . . .

'But I wrote out a summary,' I went on doggedly, 'of everything we found. I'm going to give it to her after the cross-examination. That will bring it all back.'

'And what makes you think,' she cut in, 'that she'll take it from you?'

'Oh!' My spoon fell onto the table with a clatter. 'I didn't think of that!'

'Just stay on track.'

The hearing this time was not in the jail, but in the High Court, a sprawling warren full of cubbyholes, and lawyers going about their business looking like brisk, earnest penguins.

We followed Ramya across a large courtyard and up a few flights of stairs and into a covered balcony that wound its way around the building and overlooked the central courtyard. Just outside a wooden door at the end of the balcony we stopped. Ramya checked the number she had noted on a piece of paper and nodded. She signalled to us to sit on one of the benches that lined the wall.

'*This* is the courtroom?' I asked in dismay. It looked like a clerk's room in a dreary government office block.

'Yes.'

We hunkered down to wait, and I stared out at the sky.

Half an hour later, the door opened and a clerk appeared

and nodded to Ramya. She got up and went into the room with Anoop. The door closed behind them.

Jaafer-bhai and I sat in companionable silence for a while. Then I heard him clear his throat. I turned and found him gazing at me.

'Madam, something I have been wondering.'

'Yes?'

'I am wondering how it is you are doing this work. I mean, how you decide to help these boys.'

The boys! All of a sudden I could see them again, as they had looked in the courtroom in Sabarmati jail, holding the bars and reaching out to me with eager expectant smiles. Boys. Not just pieces of paper that I had to analyze. I frowned.

'I mean, Madam, for me it is different. My own brother is in the jail.' He paused. 'Not *real* brother . . .'

His cousin. I nodded.

'So many Muslim boys are in the jail. I think almost 250. Means: for me, is something personal. For Ramya Madam, she is lawyer. But you?'

I searched through my mind looking for the answer.

'Sorry if I ask bad question.'

'No-no, Jaafer-bhai. It isn't that.' I paused to think. 'It's a good question. But I've been so busy thinking of how to give a clever answer to this in court that I haven't really asked myself what the *real* answer is!'

'Hmm . . . You are human rights activist?'

'I know a lot of human rights activists.' I shrugged. 'I generally agree with them on everything, but I don't think that's why I'm doing this.'

He tilted his head and looked at me for a long moment. Then he flashed a broad smile. 'I think . . . maybe you are enjoying.'

'You know? You may be right! I've really enjoyed this work! But . . .'

'But?'

I stopped in my tracks. 'I mean, I had no idea, when I took this on, that I would be doing crazy things like mocking up a confession on video. And meeting people like you. Sorry,' I shook my head. 'Must be some other reason.'

He leaned back, brought his hands together making a tent with his fingers. 'This is good time to think,' he decided. 'After all, only waiting. Good for time-pass. Maybe should think about your college in Delhi.'

Suddenly the sky vanished. I was back in a dim corridor that was completely enclosed, with offices on both sides. The walls were government-cream, and I was rushing to a faculty meeting. I was late. I entered the conference room quietly and slipped into a chair far from the action. The voices droned on around me, and my mind wandered off . . .

A door opened with a click, and I was back in Ahmedabad. Anoop came out of the courtroom and sat down quietly on the bench.

Ramya stuck her head out and called to Jaafer-bhai.

'Come.'

He stood up to his full height and grandly stepped into the little courtroom.

Silence.

Jaafer-bhai's question echoed in my mind. Why was I

interested in this case? He didn't waste time suggesting that I might be doing it out of the goodness of my heart. He saw at once that I felt drawn to the case because I found something about it interesting. A change from the sameness of my days at the university. I was enjoying, as he put it. And I was actually doing something useful for a change.

A war zone . . .

I was in a war zone, a place where normal time did not apply. Or an operation theatre, a scalpel in my hand, and a dedicated team at my back, the kind of team that would not give up as soon as the first problem arose. A team that was ready to work all night, if necessary. When did I ever get that kind of cooperation on my academic projects?

I had done something like this once before, in Delhi. With Ramya. And it had started out exactly the same: I had said yes because I trusted her. Trusted her partly out of contempt for the other side, a posse of drones just following orders. And there had been no one else to do the analysis. The sense of challenge and excitement had come later, as I got immersed in the work. I had gone into the courtroom smug and confident, ready to spout statistics.

And then I had turned and seen men in shackles being brought in.

The accused. Looking at me with the same sunny, hopeful expressions that I had seen on the boys behind the bars in the Sabarmati jail.

Jaafer-bhai was right: I was enjoying. Sitting on this second-floor balcony on the edge of real life, I could feel the same heady adrenaline rush. A smell of combat. Life was so full of flat sensible plains that times like these stood out like mountain peaks. When your whole life rewound and played back, these were the only moments that really came into focus.

A soft click and the door opened again.

Jaafer-bhai came out looking pleased with himself and sat down next to me on the bench.

My turn.

Ramya stuck her head out the door and raised an eyebrow at me.

'Come.'

16

Adil followed Vijay into his living room and looked around him in surprise. All the pictures were gone from the walls, leaving only dusty outlines where they had been. The books too were gone from the shelves, along with all the little Ganesh statues. Wooden crates and cardboard boxes were everywhere, half-loaded with clothes, utensils and office files. A stack of folded khaki shirts and trousers stood next to an empty box.

'Sorry about the mess,' Vijay waved a hand dismissively.

'You are . . . shifting, sir?'

'I'll tell you. But first I want to hear about your Boards.'

'They went all right, I think. I will pass. No problem. And I have got a job. In a video studio. They are taking me on as a camera attendant.'

'What!' Vijay's eyebrows shot up. 'I thought you were planning to go to college?'

'I am, sir. But I don't think I will have my results in time for admission this year. And I know I am going to like this job.' He looked around the room again. 'Where are you shifting to?'

'I'm going on transfer. To a place called Shabari Dham.'

Adil looked blank. Shabari Dham?

'It's in the Dangs forest.' Vijay's lips twisted in an ironic smile. 'I think you could call this a banwaas. You know that word? Banwaas?'

'I know about the Ramayan, sir. Banwaas is exile: when Ram is sent away to the forest. They are sending you away from Ahmedabad ... because of what you did? During the riots?'

'More likely because of what I didn't do. I didn't cooperate.' Vijay paused a moment. 'That doesn't worry me too much. I expected this, at least.' Another pause. 'What worries me more is what they plan to do once all of us are out of the way, the officers who didn't support the riots.' He shook his head. 'I can predict that they are going to go through all the files and try to clean up the record: for when they have to produce the documents relating to those days. Because there is definitely going to be an enquiry.'

'How is your mother, Adil?' Vijay's wife came into the living room with two mugs of chai. She set one down in front of Adil and handed the other one to Vijay.

'She is much better, Auntie. Almost back to normal. She and Faiza are coming back beginning of June. For the monsoon term. Amma thinks she will be able to go back to work by then.'

'Oh! We will miss them.'

'When are you leaving, Auntie?'

'Soon, Adil, we have to go soon. Maybe next week.'

The doorbell rang, and she got up to let in some friends

who had come to say goodbye. Adil sat back and slipped into a dream, let the sounds of their conversation wash over him, warm and receding into the distance.

He looked out the window. A cloudless blue sky. Trees bathed in a gentle late-afternoon light, the shadow of Vijay's house creeping slowly up their trunks until only their top branches were golden and bright. There was something about such an impossibly beautiful day that made him sad.

Like a September sky, he thought, clear and bright and empty. Something is over. The blessings of a monsoon. A season in my life is coming to an end.

He decided to sit still and hold on tight to the moment, sip his tea and store up all his memories in the form of images, images that he could replay and relive slowly in the lonely evenings at home.

Ten days before Amma and Faiza were due to return, the city of Ahmedabad was rocked by a series of bomb blasts.

Makeshift bombs. Nothing big. Nobody died. But a few people were injured.

Everybody froze.

Who . . .?

In the newspapers, on television, images of bombs that failed to go off.

Adil and his friends met in the evenings in his home and spoke in whispers, bracing themselves for the violence that was sure to come. Godhra, they would say. After Godhra came the riots. What is going to happen to us now?

But days passed and nothing happened. And no one was even arrested.

Adil held his breath.

It was Faiza who broke the tension, bounding onto the scene like a Rottweiler with Amma in tow. '*Useless* terrorists!' she fumed. 'Putting piddly little bombs on buses to hurt who-knows-who! Even *I* know who they should have killed!'

'Faiza!' Amma gasped.

'Amma!' she retorted. '*Everyone* knows who did what in the riots. So why did they have to go and do something stupid like this? Only *asking* for trouble!'

'Well, there has been no trouble,' Amma said mildly.

'That is what is so confusing,' Adil broke in. 'I mean, all of us thought that there was going to be violence. Or arrests. But nothing has happened. Almost like . . . the police are not concerned.'

'Why should they be concerned?' Faiza rounded on him savagely. '*They* only would have done it!'

'Faiza! What are you saying!'

'Amma! You don't *know*! They *couldn't* have done the riots if the police didn't help! And government doesn't care. What is so bad if a few people get hurt? It's okay, if the whole world starts to think that Muslim people are terrorists.'

'*Why* do we have to be like this?' Amma wailed, looking at Adil for support. 'Why can't we just be peaceful together?'

Faiza gave her a baleful look.

'No, really,' Amma went on. 'Today I had to go to the Old City. And in Khadia I saw something amazing. In one of the pols, I saw a dog and a cat drinking milk from the same dish! Can you imagine? If a dog and a cat can be friends like that, why is it that people have all these problems?'

'Amma! I was there with you, remember? And I saw that dog and cat too. I don't think they were friends, like you are saying. In fact, the dog and the cat did not even *look* at each other. They just kept their heads down and drank.'

'I am not saying that they have to be friends, Faiza. Maybe that is too much to expect. But at least they were not fighting, the way dogs and cats do. And that is a positive thing.'

'No,' Faiza went on doggedly. 'It is just the milk. If the man wasn't giving them milk, they wouldn't be there at all. Or they would be fighting. It is all because of the milk.'

'Well, there is no one to give us milk like that.' Amma shrugged, dismissing the thought.

'No, Amma,' Adil said softly. 'On this thing you are wrong. I think there *is* a man with all the milk to give us. And when he gets tired of all the violence, *that* is what he is going to do.'

'Yes,' Faiza went on like an oracle. 'And that is the worst part. Because then we are all going to behave like dogs and cats: *so* happy to be getting all this milk for nothing that we will just put our heads down and drink. We will forget. We will be peaceful. We will say everything is okay.' She paused for breath, and looked around at Adil and his friends. 'And whoever gets the most milk, he will even say this man is God.'

Amma shook her head.

'But, in truth, he is no kind of God. It is we only who have turned into dogs and cats.' Faiza paused, geared up for her last pronouncement. 'And he will be the master of all of us!'

17

And so it went. The rest of the year was without incident, and the next year promised to continue in this blessed calm. Adil kept his head down and worked, learnt his new trade.

Sohail began to seek him out as his choice of camera assistant, and Adil would watch him closely as he framed his shots and caught what was special about the light. Soon he had graduated from being just a camera attendant to doing the camera work for simple shoots with news teams.

Then one day near the end of March, when the temperatures had begun to soar again, the peace was shattered by the news that a government minister had been shot and killed.

An ordinary Brahmin with a conscience.

The words floated to the top of Adil's mind, taking him back to that night in Vijay's living room. Adil remembered the voice of a man who had been there, at the secret meeting called the night before the riots started. A man who knew everything. Who had been ready to talk. A man who was sure that they would think a thousand times before they touched him.

The minister who had been killed had already gone on his own and deposed before the Special Investigation Team, the tribunal investigating the riots. So they would never have let him out of their sight.

Vijay, Adil thought, suddenly remembering the other man of conscience. Thank God Vijay is not here!

Adil was booked to go with a news team to Law Garden to get the story. They arrived late in the afternoon and set up. He removed the lens cap and looked into the viewfinder. In the frame was a face with eyes he knew at once. Adil's head jerked up: he was certain he was seeing things.

'Faiza's brother!' she burst out.

He stood and stared.

'I'm sorry,' she went on, 'I guess you don't remember me.'

'Megha,' he mumbled. 'You're Megha . . .'

'Oh, right,' she gave a rueful smile. 'You've heard my name. Well, I don't know yours.'

'It's Adil. Adil Ansari.' A silence. 'I thought you might be a journalist.'

'I'm not! I'm a student.'

'A student?'

'Film and video.'

Adil nodded, remembering his first shoot on Dumas Beach.

The producer strolled by. 'We got here early,' he mused. 'We have to wait.'

'Enough time for some chai?' Megha asked.

He shrugged.

'Come!' she called to Adil and headed for a chaiwala who was sitting under a tree with his kettle.

They sat down on the ground with their tiny cups of chai. She wore jeans and a short kurta. Today there was no dupatta, and her hair was pulled back into a makeshift knot.

He looked away.

She read his mind at once. 'Oh! I usually don't wear a dupatta, especially when it's this hot.'

'N-no . . .' Adil was suddenly embarrassed. 'It's not that. It's just that I was remembering that you had a peach-coloured dupatta that day.'

'Well, I *was* going into a disturbed area.'

'Why? What made you come?'

'I wanted to see for myself.' A pause. 'That day I wasn't on campus, I was at my LG's place . . .'

'LG?'

'Local guardian. Lucky for me. Because they had locked the gates to the Institute. No one could come in, and students couldn't go out. They wouldn't even open the gates to let in the bais who washed our clothes. They had to face the mobs.' Another pause. 'Well, I wanted to go to the Old City. I asked my LG if I could take his car: the ricks wouldn't go. He wasn't happy, but he let me go. And he gave me one piece of advice: to say I was from SEWA.'

Adil smiled. 'I guessed you weren't.'

She frowned. 'How?'

'You didn't even speak Gujarati.' A pause. 'Where did you learn Urdu?'

'Urdu?'

'You were speaking Urdu all the time.'

She thought a moment. 'I guess I was. Well, I learnt it in school.'

'You went to an Urdu school?'

'No! I had to choose an additional Indian language, Urdu, Tamil, Bengali or Gujarati. I chose Urdu: I thought it would be the easiest: except for the script, it's pretty much the same as Hindi. And the new words were sort of familiar. I had heard them before. I just didn't know what they meant.' A pause. 'What about you? Where did *you* learn Urdu?'

'My mother is an Urdu teacher.'

She paused. 'I was going to ask you about her. Your sister had said you were looking for her that day. What happened?'

He hesitated. 'We found her, a couple of days later. She was in hospital, unconscious. Someone had hit her on the head. But she's all right now.'

'I'm so sorry about this, Adil!' she looked up at him imploringly.

Guilt . . .

'It's not your fault!' He burst out. He hesitated, decided to go on. 'You were upset, that day. I remember. Like you felt, well, responsible for the riots because you suddenly remembered you were a Hindu.'

Her eyes opened wide. 'Is *that* what you thought! I saw you looking at me. But no: for your information, I am *not* a Hindu.'

'No? Then what . . .'

'I'm not *anything*! I guess you don't know what I mean.'

'No, I do. The person who saved our lives during the riots is like that. I heard someone call him a secularist.'

'That's not the same thing. A secularist is just someone who believes that religion has no place in politics, or in government. When I say I'm not anything, what I mean is that I am an atheist. I don't believe in God at all.'

He sat back and tried to take in the enormity of her words. 'Why not?'

'Adil, ever since I was a kid, I've been seeing riots on TV. And all the time it has something to do with religion. One day I asked myself if religion had any use at all, except to get people killed from time to time. I decided that it didn't.' A pause. 'And then that day I heard my name being called out like that. I realized that my *name* had a religion behind it. That I wasn't free at all.'

Adil felt his head spin at the sudden overload. He was in a bewildering new world with endless vistas, all unexplored. A world where having a religion meant not being free.

A world with no God.

'You *are* free . . .' he began.

'No. Not really. I can just see myself falling in line, and living out a safe, secure, *boring* life when there is a bigger world waiting out there! A *different* world! Where you can be anything you want to be!'

Her eyes were glowing, Adil thought. As though they could really see further into the distance. See a bigger brighter world.

'But isn't that where you are going?' He hesitated. 'Abroad?'

She shook her head. 'That isn't the other world I meant! I think I'm looking for a world I lost, somewhere.' She paused, her gaze turning inward. 'A world that was *real*. I remember sitting with my grandfather when I was a child. He was always reading newspapers,' she went on. 'And his newspapers were in Urdu. When he was young, all our men learnt Urdu and Persian, but women were educated only in Hindi. And the men ate Muslim food and behaved like nawabs, but women were vegetarian. That was how it was back then.' She paused, picked up the thread again. 'I wanted to get inside his world. But whenever I asked him to teach me to read like him, he would laugh and tell me that times had changed. Why? From what he said, those days were . . . better. As though the air was . . . clearer. There was a sense of . . . *grace.*'

Adil had a sudden flash frame of the letdown he had felt on Dumas Beach, when the last shot was over. As though the real world was, in some sense, over-exposed. That the light inside the frame had been more exquisite.

'So when I had the chance in school to opt for Urdu, I did.'

'I am not so sure my world is all that bright,' Adil remarked. 'It would be . . . stifling for someone like you. I see it as a lot of dark corners.' He paused. 'And a lot of religion.'

'Like my name,' she mused. 'It doesn't matter if I *say* I am an atheist. My name marks me, and puts me in a box.'

'Maybe.' Then a sudden thought: 'Who gave you your name, Megha?'

She smiled wistfully. 'My mother. And she didn't mean it to be . . . anything in particular. It's just that I was born the day the monsoon came. She saw that first cloud, leading a whole bank of rain clouds. And all of a sudden the breeze was cool.' She tilted her head and looked at up Adil. 'So she named me after that cloud.'

'Monsoon-Megh,' he smiled, 'who brings the rain.'

'Yes!' she beamed. 'The first monsoon cloud.' She paused for effect. 'The *promise* of rain.'

They returned their cups and ambled back to the camera. The daylight had begun to fade, and the attendant had brought out the lights.

'Here,' the producer thrust an extension board into his hand. 'See if you can get this thing to work.'

Adil put it down on the ground and took a screwdriver out of his pocket. He opened it up and saw that a wire was broken.

Then he heard the click of a camera, felt the flash. Looked up.

Another flash caught him full frontal with the screwdriver in one hand and the opened up extension board in the other.

The man put down the camera and gave him a grim smile, his eyes cold and reptilian. Then he got up and calmly walked away.

Adil stood there in a daze. The extension board slipped out of his hand and crashed to the ground.

'Adil! Ready?' Megha's voice broke in on the turmoil in his mind.

He turned away from the darkness and back towards the light.

After pack up, Adil made his way home in a happy daze, replaying and reliving his time with Megha. He remembered her eyes, glowing in the slanted rays of the evening sun. They would follow him into his dreams, he thought.

He felt his cell phone ring in his pocket. He took it out and looked at the display.

Megha.

'Hi,' he ventured.

'Hi, Adil.' A pause. 'I'm in a rick, on the way to my LG's place, and . . . well, I wanted to be in touch with someone. For safety. In case he takes a wrong turn, and I need to let someone know where I am. You don't mind, do you? Talking to me?'

'Of course not!' Adil burst out. 'I am an *idiot*! I should have dropped you! Why didn't you ask me to?'

'No-no,' she assured him. 'No need for that. And this place is generally safe. It's just that nowadays I don't like to take chances. You don't know who is who. Who did what last year.' A pause. 'And if he sees me talking to someone, he isn't so likely to get ideas.'

'He?'

'He understands that much English, Adil.'

'Oh. The driver.' A pause. 'But Megh, I think you left something here!'

'What!'

'Tell him you forgot something here. That you have to come back.'

'But . . .'

'And I'll be waiting here for you. Hurry!'

'Bhaiya!' He heard her cry out to the driver. A flurry of instructions. 'Right, Adil. I'm coming . . .'

'Don't hang up!'

'No . . .'

In a few minutes, a rick found his and stopped. She got out, paid the driver off, and came running towards his rick and climbed in beside him.

'Hi again!' she smiled up at him.

'Megh . . .' he breathed.

The driver looked around for directions.

'Want to go and have kebabs?' he improvised.

'No, Adil. I think they're expecting me. You don't mind coming with me? To my LG's place?'

'No, but we're going out together next time, okay?'

'It's a date!' She flashed him a brilliant smile and they were off.

She guided the driver to a quiet residential neighbourhood and they stopped outside a bungalow with a garden in front. She led him under some tall trees to the front door and rang the bell. A grey-haired gentleman opened the door.

'Hi, Uncle!' she beamed at her LG. 'This is Adil. He insisted on escorting me home.'

'Well, come in, both of you!'

She took Adil's hand and led him in. Motioned to him to sit beside her.

'So you're a student at the Institute with Megha?'

'No, Uncle,' Megha cut in. 'Adil is a cameraman. We'd met before, and today he was doing the camera for the story we were covering at Law Garden.'

The LG frowned. 'You look a little young to be a cameraman.'

Adil nodded. 'I was planning to go to college, but I did not have my results in time last year. So I just continued my summer job in the studio, and started doing shoots by myself. But I have admission for this monsoon term.'

The LG nodded. 'To study what?'

'Chemistry. But I like this work, so I think I will take it up again later.'

'Adil has a feel for gadgets,' Megha turned to look at him warmly.

'Why don't you stay for dinner? We're just putting it on the table.'

'No, sir. I've kept my rick waiting. My mother is expecting me. But thank you.'

'Well, next time. Glad to meet you.'

Megha led him to the front door and gave him a brief hug. 'Thanks, Adil. See you soon.'

It probably meant nothing to her, he thought as he got back into the rick. But he felt himself tingle at having been so close to her. He thought of her eyes, how she had looked up at him as they sat together, and slipped back into his reverie . . .

I will see her eyes in my dreams tonight, he thought.

But the eyes he saw in his dreams that night were not hers. They were ghoul's eyes, cold and dark and pitiless. He was back in Shah Alam cemetery, and this time he was alone. It was sunset. The graves opened, one by one, and they emerged in slow motion. He heard a click, saw the flash as they captured his soul. He tried to turn and run, but his legs would not move. Then they came for him, stretched out their long, long arms to hold him and drag him back with them into a bottomless pit . . .

He opened his mouth to scream . . .

And then the room was full of light. Amma was there at his bedside, her hand on his brow checking to see if he had fever.

'Just a bad dream,' he muttered. His pulse began to slow down. He took a deep breath, looked around.

Faiza came into the room and sat on the edge of his bed.

'What did you dream about?' she asked.

He hesitated. She held his gaze, willing him to tell her.

'I was back in the graveyard. Shah Alam. The graves opened, and the ghouls came out and started to drag me back into the pit with them.'

She shuddered. 'Better be careful, Bhai,' she said. 'When the ghosts leave the graves it means that something bad is going to happen.' She shuddered again. 'Run away! Now. Tonight. Go where they will never find you!'

'Faiza!' Amma cried from the doorway. 'It was just a dream! Leave him alone, now.' She turned. 'Adil, you have been working too hard. I think you are over-tired. Come, Faiza. Let him go back to sleep.'

She reached for the light switch.

'Leave it on, Amma,' he mumbled. 'It will help me to forget the dream . . .'

18

They packed up the shoot by mid-afternoon and she followed
him back to the studio to return the camera and the reflectors.
She sat on one of the plastic chairs, waiting for him to be
done, and opened the sketchpad she carried, glancing at some
of the storyboards she had done a while ago.

'You like to draw your shots first?' his voice floated in on
her thoughts.

She shook her head. 'No. I don't do it any more. But I had
been thinking of going for animation. Once. And this is
always the first step with an animated film.' She looked up at
him. 'I still like the idea of planning out frames like this.
Letting the story tell me the right shot pattern.'

She got up and followed him out of the studio. Now they
were free, walking past the Paldi Bus Terminal, heading for
her Institute.

'I think you see it as a whole film before you even start.
You even know how you are going to edit later.'

'And you don't?'

'I am not supposed to.' He shrugged. 'I have to do what the
director wants.'

'But what about *you*?' she persisted. 'What excites you about camera work?'

'Me?' He paused to think. 'I guess . . . it would be . . . light!' he pronounced enigmatically, waving his hand in the air like a magician.

'So you're attracted to light!' she smiled.

'I suppose so,' he agreed. 'I started out helping another cameraman, and what I liked most was seeing how he caught the quality of light. Things I thought would be impossible to capture. Once he even got village women to hang up their saris along a wall, and then he turned the reflectors on them to light the shot.' He paused to smile, and looked at her wonderingly. 'Or the way *your* eyes glow in the slant rays of the evening sun, just like a cat's! They are amazing!'

'You're like a moth,' she murmured.

'A moth? That reminds me of a song we had to learn in school when I was a child. A prayer. There was a moth that was attracted to the light.'

Zindagi ho meri parwaane ki soorat, ya rab
Ilm ki shama se ho mujhko muhabbat, ya rab,

'How do *you* know it?' he burst out.

'Silly! They teach it in so many schools!'

'And you know what it means?'

'Of course! "May my life be like the face of the moth, oh Lord, May I be full of love for the flame of knowledge."'

'No.'

She paused mid-step. 'No?'

'No,' he repeated softly. '*In* love.'

'But . . .'

'The moth is in love with the flame.'

A moment of stillness. He saw her eyes widen as she turned to stare at him. *In* love . . .

Her hand slipped shyly into his and he threaded his fingers through hers, and they walked on oblivious to the world of Ahmedabad around them.

They entered the National Institute of Design campus by the main gate and were enveloped by its grand trees and lush green lawns, a dream space that was a world apart from the town he knew. Megha let go of his hand and forged ahead, leaving him to follow.

There were young people everywhere, all his age, with no adults in sight. Many of the boys had long hair. Everyone seemed to be wearing torn jeans and wild, colourful clothes. Hanging around in groups. Couples lost in a world of their own, sitting under the shady trees and looking into each other's eyes. He followed Megha and they joined a group sitting around one young man with a guitar.

'Who's your friend, Megha?'

'Guys, this is Adil. He's the cameraman in the group I'm attached to. We packed up early, so we decided to come here.'

'A cameraman? Impossible! You said you wouldn't be caught dead with a cameraman!'

Adil stared at her in surprise.

'I changed my mind!' she exclaimed, turning to the guy with the guitar and glowering at him. 'He's different! Not like *you*! A guy holding onto a tool like it's the phallic end of the unit! He actually let me take some of the shots today!'

'The . . . *what*?' Adil gulped.

'It's true, Adil!' she protested. 'You have to *see* how they get on! One day I was on a set, and they were filming a young actress. And the cameraman kept twirling the focus at her. In and out, in and out, over and over again, while the shot was getting ready.' She shook her head. 'She knew what he meant by it, but she had to stand there and take it.'

Adil paused. 'I have heard some of them talk like that, after a shoot, the cameramen and the light boys. Most of these men have never had a chance to talk to a woman. Not in their whole lives. They have no idea what to say to her.'

Megha frowned. 'But still . . .'

'They feel that all girls are going to brush them off. So they settle for getting them bugged. Getting any sort of reaction, I think.'

'But if we even smile back, the same men think we are easy,' Megha added. 'And then they despise us. They only respect women who treat them like they are nothing.'

'*Nooooo*, Megha!' the guitar man broke in. 'You're exaggerating, as usual!'

'I'm not saying *you* . . .' she reached down and patted his head.

'Go away,' the guitar man growled. 'Show your friend the campus.'

She led Adil towards the main building. The entire ground floor was a high-ceilinged open space supported by grand concrete pillars. Large clay sculptures stood here and there, to the side of the walkway, set off by smooth white river stones.

'He likes you,' Adil said suddenly.

She shrugged. 'He'll get over it.'

They turned at the end of the corridor and were back in the sunlight. Adil blinked. Was it as easy as that? Was everything different from how he had always imagined?

Then he heard the familiar sound of the evening azaan from Jamalpur mosque, across the river. He turned his head in surprise.

'What?' Megha looked up at him.

'I was just beginning to wonder how many of the things I always believed, since I was a child, how many of them were true. And right at that moment . . .' he shook his head, 'the biggest thing of all.'

She gave him a long look. 'And? What do you think?'

'I don't know,' he admitted. 'I don't know anymore. But all of a sudden the world looks . . . huge.'

'And brighter,' she smiled.

'Yes . . .'

She nodded. A quick glance at the sky. 'Let's go. There's one more place here that I want to show you.'

'Where?' he murmured. She was so close. His pulse began to beat hard in his throat.

'My hostel! I want to show you where I live!' She turned to go. 'Come, Adil.'

Come, Adil . . .

There was a buzz in the air. A live current sang in his veins.

She turned and smiled at him, her eyes reflecting back the golden rays of the evening sun.

And in a daze he started to follow her across the cool green lawn. Gliding. Light as air. Like a moth hopelessly in love with the light.

19

I followed Ramya into the little courtroom. Heard the soft click behind me as someone closed the door.

The light was brighter in this little room, brighter than it had been in the jail. And everything this time was in close-up. The judge's bench faced the door, and was relatively smaller and only slightly raised. The walls enclosed us like parentheses.

The judge gave me a warm smile of recognition. To her right, Mr Verma also looked up expectantly.

I smiled at him. He nodded back solemnly.

Ramya indicated an empty chair just below the judge's bench, to the left. I sat down, and she took a seat right next to me.

'You swear to tell the truth . . .' the judge fast-forwarded.

'Yes,' I replied looking around. On the other side of Ramya was a man I didn't know, or hadn't registered last time, a man dressed in legal-looking clothes. He must be the prosecutor, I guessed.

The judge nodded at him. 'You may proceed.'

He cleared his throat, peered down into his notes. 'Deepaben . . . Ms Sahai . . .' he hesitated.

'Dr Sahai is fine,' I put in.

He looked up at me in surprise. Out of the corner of my eye I caught a look of amusement flitting across the judge's face.

'In this context,' I clarified. 'I mean, if we met at a party you should certainly call me Deepa-ben. But since I'm here as an expert witness, it's better to keep my qualifications in focus. I hope that's all right with you.'

'It's fine!' he muttered.

I took a deep breath and braced myself.

'Right, Dr Sahai. Let us start with that only. You are a linguist?'

'Yes.'

He paused and nodded. Looked at his notes again. 'And, as I understand it, a linguist is someone who knows a number of languages?'

'No,' I replied firmly.

The whole world around us ground to a halt. Freeze frame.

The prosecutor unfroze first. Frowned. Looked down at his notes.

Mr Verma sat back and put his pencil down. For the first time since I had met him, he seemed to be smiling.

'What do you mean, "no"?'

'I mean that what you just said is not correct. A linguist is *not* someone who simply knows many languages. In fact, some of the best-known linguists in the US only know one language. Or two.'

He looked down at his notes again.

He'd based his whole line of questioning on this, I suddenly rcalized. That I'm supposed to be a linguist, but that I couldn't possibly know Gujarati well enough to have analyzed the confessions as an expert!

'Then could you please enlighten the court as to what exactly a linguist is?' he asked resentfully, trapped into asking a question that gave me back the advantage.

I nodded. 'I will.' I looked around. Everyone was looking at me curiously. Mr Verma picked up his pencil and leaned forward. 'To put it simply, a linguist is someone who looks at language. Language: as opposed to languages. Language is the best window into how human thought is organized. Some linguists focus on this aspect of language: how it constitutes a software, as it were, for facilitating human thought, allowing us to demarcate concepts and manipulate them. We believe that language is genetic: all children exposed to language before the age of five do manage to learn it. Some linguists look at how children acquire language. And some try to discover what this genetic grammar inside the mind might look like.' I paused again. 'Some also look at how languages change over time, are born, die. And some look at how the same language might be spoken differently by different groups within a society.'

'And which of these aspects applies here?'

'Well, I am interested in analyzing recorded language data. I've done a lot of research on people giving verbatim testimony. So I know what normal human speech looks like. In other words, I can make out at once when a corpus of speech does *not* fit the pattern.' I paused again. 'I have also developed a way of expressing this deviance in quantitative terms.'

He frowned.

'Of course,' I went on, 'the actual data corpora this time were in Gujarati.'

'Can you spell corpora?' Mr Verma's voice came at me from the far end of the judge's bench.

I looked up in surprise. 'C-O-R-P-O-R-A,' I spelt the word slowly for him. 'That's the plural of corpus. Corpus means "body". A chunk of speech.'

He nodded, and started writing again.

'As I was saying, I can follow Gujarati a bit, but I can't say I really *know* it. So I took help to read and understand the confession statements. I took help from two professional scribes who work in Gujarati every day. And for comparison purposes, I videotaped depositions on a similar topic by two similar boys in Gujarati, with the same scribes writing down their testimony in real time. In the same frame.' I paused, and looked up at the judge. 'I gave you a copy of the tape and the transcripts last time.'

She nodded. 'I have them.'

The prosecutor looked down at his notes and turned the page.

'I believe you have done this sort of work before?' he asked, looking up at me.

'Yes.'

He waited for me to elaborate.

'Where?' he asked, finally.

'In Delhi.'

'A similar case?'

'No, the confessions there were in English.'

He frowned. 'I mean: did that case also involve terrorism?'

'It was also a POTA case.'

He nodded. 'May I ask what you are being paid as an expert witness in this case?'

I paused. There was no point in side-stepping the question. 'It's *pro bono*. I'm not taking payment.'

'And may I ask why?'

I shrugged. 'I guess I trust Ramya. And the work is interesting.' I paused. 'And I'm not comfortable with taking money for things like this.'

He leaned forward. 'Could it be because you yourself are biased?'

'That's a classic Catch-22 situation! I won't answer the question.'

He paused. Reframed. 'Could it be that you yourself are anti-national?'

I jerked my head up sharply. 'I resent . . .'

'Just answer "yes" or "no"!'

I looked around desperately, caught the judge's eye. 'Your Honour, can we do without all the Perry Mason stuff?'

Next to me Ramya stirred. 'Your Honour,' she said softly to the judge, with a smile that did not reach her eyes, 'I would never badger an expert witness. I always give them a chance to explain themselves.'

The judge nodded, turned and looked at me. 'Yes, Dr Sahai. You may take your time and answer. And I would also like to know what you mean when you say "a classic Catch-22 situation".'

I took a deep breath. 'A Catch-22 situation is one where

you can only prove you are an unbiased witness by actually not being a witness at all. If I take payment for this work, it makes me a mercenary, and therefore biased. And if I *don't* take payment, that makes me *a priori* a supporter, and therefore biased. According to this reasoning, in order to be unbiased I would have to *not* be a witness for the defence.' I stopped and waited for Mr Verma to finish with the sentence. Then I looked up at the judge and continued, 'So given that I *am* an expert witness for the defence, and not for the prosecution, what answer could I possibly give about accepting payment that would show me to be unbiased?'

'And your response to the other question?' the judge asked.

I nodded. 'The term "anti-national" . . . I think there is an assumption here that we agree about what that means.' I paused. 'Is a nationalist someone who simply agrees with everything the central or state government does? I don't think so: governments come and go. So is a nationalist someone who supports a party that claims to represent the majority community?' I shrugged dismissively. 'And what do we mean when we say the nation? Which group represents the nation? The majority community? The upper-middle class? The upper castes? Men?'

'How is this relevant . . .' the prosecutor broke in.

I turned back to the judge. 'Your Honour, can I complete what I was saying?'

'If it is relevant,' she said.

'It is. You see, if we regard India as fundamentally plural, we have to expect a number of equally valid views about what is "national". These are all, in my opinion, biases. In linguistics, we believe that simply having language forces us to perceive the world in a biased fashion, as primary input gets slotted into categories that might be seen as arbitrary by non-human intelligence. You can't avoid that, but you *can* try to be open about what your bias is.' A pause. 'So I want to clarify my bias.'

'Go on.'

'I don't see this country as an extension of myself. I see it as something far more diverse than that, where minorities are not aberrations, but part of the basic nature of the place. So when I agree to help defend someone from outside the mainstream, I don't see that as something anti-national. No. I should not be looking at that sort of thing at all! In fact, if someone in trouble could only be helped by someone from his own community that would be a very strong signal that his community did not have a place in the Indian mainstream. And *that*, I think, would be truly anti-national. According to *my* version of "national".'

'Interesting,' the judge remarked noncommittally. 'Now, if you don't mind, there is something I want to ask you.'

'Yes.' I braced for a change of topic.

'To go back to the confessions, you said last time that the handwriting did not look like it could have been written at sixty words per minute.'

I nodded. 'I have never seen longhand done at sixty words per minute.'

'Then what would you say would have been the speed of the handwriting?'

Jaafer-bhai, I thought, remembering his second

transcription, the neater one. 'We have a timed transcription that is similar to the handwriting in the confessions. Our faster scribe was asked to re-transcribe what he had done, from the videotape. He was asked to use the pause button, and was allowed to rewind the tape if necessary to review a phrase. I wanted to get a truly verbatim transcription, repetitions and all. Without any shortening or paraphrase. The handwriting is more or less as neat as the handwriting in the confessions.'

'What was the speed?'

'The speed of that transcription was eighteen words per minute.'

I rummaged in my folder and produced a Xerox copy of the transcription Jaafer-bhai had taken down off the videotape and handed it to her. Then I glimpsed a spare copy of his other transcription, done in real time, the ratty-looking one full of scratches and abbreviations. I held it up too, to emphasize the difference. 'And this is the one he did at forty-six words per minute. You already have a copy of this.'

She nodded thoughtfully. 'Are you saying, then, that the actual confessions would have been written at eighteen words per minute?'

I hesitated. 'You are asking me for my opinion here. I was not there when the actual confessions were recorded. And it is also possible that taking down dictation off a videotape is not exactly the same thing.'

'Yes. I am asking for your opinion,' the judge confirmed.

'Then . . . I would say that the speed of the transcription of the confessional statements would have been somewhere between twenty and twenty-two words per minute. Definitely not more than twenty-five.' I paused. 'As I said earlier, there is no way that these confessions could have been obtained in the manner in which the police are claiming.' I opened my file and took out the summary I had made and handed it to her. 'Your Honour, I have summarized my findings here, since my deposition is of a technical nature.'

She nodded, and took the stapled pages from me. I breathed a sigh of relief and got ready to leave.

'Wait!' The prosecutor seized back the initiative. 'I have one last question.'

I turned and looked at him. Waited.

'Since you can tell all this from the look of the confessions, and you say that they were not taken in the manner that the police are saying, could you tell the court how exactly these confessions would have been taken?'

Alarm bells began to ring inside my head as I saw the golden trap. *Torture* . . . the word screamed silently in the little courtroom. But to say it out loud would be to go way beyond my brief.

I shook my head to dispel the image and smiled enigmatically. 'I will have to leave that to your imagination. I'm sure you know the Gujarat police better than I do.'

Jaafer-bhai, Anoop and I followed Ramya back down the stairs and into the courtyard, which suddenly seemed narrower, darker, more confining.

An old bearded Muslim man with a distraught expression walked up to me holding a photograph of a young man. 'Madam, mera beta bhi jail mein hai.'

Behind him, a number of other old Muslim men were holding legal-looking documents. Some of them also held photographs: sons who must also be in jail. They were watching us closely and getting ready to come forward too. I stopped.

'No!' Ramya barked. 'You don't know them! Come!'

I gave them an apologetic look and hurried after Ramya.

'What's wrong?' I asked.

'What did you think you were up to in there?' she snarled, all her tension rearing up and flattening me like a tsunami. 'I *told* you to stay with the confessions. But no! If the judge hadn't brought it up at the end, you would have gone on and on, on your own trip!' She rounded on Jaafer-bhai. 'And you! All you did was go on and on about the fantastic work you did in the Gulf. He gave you a chance to show off, and you jumped at it, feet first!' She turned to Anoop. 'He is the only one who did what he was supposed to do. He just talked about the confessions, and the work he did.' She turned back and glared at us. 'That's it! We're going to lose the case!' she concluded darkly.

'I thought the judge was very positive . . .' I began mildly.

'What do you know?' she snapped back.

'Look,' I ventured reasonably, 'I had to deal with the Prosecutor's questions, and I did keep the whole thing in the realm of linguistics.'

'That's the *point*! He was out to distract you, and you let him. *Wasted* the chance to keep the focus on the confessions. And the boys!'

I stalked off, stung by the sudden criticism. Jaafer-bhai came behind me, shaking his head.

'Not to mind, Madam,' he said soothingly. 'She is very tense, worried. Too much pressure. You must forgive!'

'No!' I snapped. 'This is . . .'

Ramya's cell phone rang. She grabbed it. 'Hello? *Who* is this? *Who* is this? . . .' Her voice rose shrilly.

'Ramya,' I said coolly, slowly, 'hang up. Hang . . . *up*!'

My voice got through the fog and she looked up and saw me in front of her. She clicked off and put the phone away. Her hand was shaking.

'They know everything that happened inside the courtroom,' she murmured.

'They?' I asked.

'Yes. I get these calls all the time.' Her expression softened as she saw the look of incomprehension on my face. 'Deepi, I'm sorry.'

'It's okay,' I said stiffly.

She shook her head. 'I can't get away from them. I can't even book a flight to Ahmedabad without them getting to know. And when I'm here, they don't leave me alone . . .'

20

The next time they came for him it was not a dream. He woke up in the dark with a feeling. His heart was pounding. And then he heard them.

Police boots tramping in the street.

Nightsticks striking the ground as they got closer.

Enough noise to wake the dead.

Laughter.

He slipped out of the living room.

'Beta?' Amma murmured sleepily. 'What is it, son?'

Faiza shot up, instantly awake. 'Under the bed! Quick! Don't even *try* to leave the house. They have got it surrounded.'

He dived into the darkness, vanished. They started banging on the front door.

Faiza leapt out of bed and ran to the living room. '*Who* is it?' she growled.

'Open the door, Pakeezah!'

'There is nobody named Pakeezah here! Wrong house!'

'Open up!'

'Do you have a warrant?'

A laugh. 'Open the door or we will break it!'

She took a deep breath. Then she opened the door a crack. They pushed her aside and strode in.

'Adil Ansari! Where is he?'

There were twenty of them. Thirty . . .

Amma appeared in the doorway. 'Who . . .?' She froze mid-step. Her gaze fell on one of the group and his nightstick and she sank to the floor with a moan, clutching the back of a chair.

He turned to her and grinned.

'Ab ki baar tu upar jayegi! Bete ko kahan chhupaya hai?'

This time you are going to die! Where have you hidden that son of yours?

Amma's eyes glazed and her face went blank.

'Amma!' Faiza screamed, running to catch her as she swayed. She turned and faced the intruders. 'You *can't* come into our house without a warrant! Go away! Leave us alone!'

From under Amma's bed, Adil heard the divan he had been sleeping on being turned over and smashed. Curtains being ripped off the windows. A chair splintered and the cupboard door swung open with a shrill creak.

The sound of booted feet heading for the bedroom.

'Get out! He is gone! He is gone where you will never find him!'

Sounds of a scuffle. Faiza howled.

And then silence.

'Aane khatam kari naakhiye?'

Finish her off! Adil came out from under the bed and rushed to the living room. 'Let her go. I am here. What do you want to ask me?'

A nightstick hit him straight in the solar plexus, below his rib cage. A booted foot struck his knee.

His breath stopped. Then his legs buckled below him and he felt himself falling. Strong hands grabbed him and held him from behind.

The moment passed. Adil looked up and saw a man he remembered, a man with the face of a large field rat. Someone from Crime Detection Branch.

'I know you, sir,' he murmured. 'What is this about?'

Another blow from a nightstick landed across his back.

'Shut up! We will ask the questions.'

In the haze, he felt handcuffs being slipped onto his wrists.

'Suno!' A voice near the floor barked. Out of the corner of his eye, he saw one of them thrust blank sheets of paper in front of Amma. 'Listen! Sign these. Now! Or you will not see your son again.'

Amma began to wail.

The man grabbed her where she sat on the floor and shook her. 'Sign! Or next time it will be Barot coming, not me. And then you will die!' He grinned. 'Time to say your prayers, mata-ji!'

Amma's eyes glazed again and she slumped in a dead faint.

'Leave her!' the man from Crime Branch barked. 'This time we have the boy. No need for father-shather brother-shudder coming in place of suspect. We can come back and get the old lady to sign later.'

Adil felt himself being propelled out the door and into the night.

'*Bhaiiiii* . . .' Faiza's voice followed behind him like a dirge.

They passed the street where Faiza had last called out to him like that. And then called him Addie-bhai to save him from the goons. The street was empty. Every door was tightly shut.

She had told him to run away. But he hadn't listened.

And now they were dragging him into their grave.

'Go and dump him in Bungalow 16,' he heard the man from Crime Branch say. 'We can do one more tonight.'

21

When he came to, he was on the floor of the room. Alone.

He tried to remember.

The first day, three of them had come and beat him with flexible canes, punched him, kicked him and thrust blank sheets of paper at him, telling him to sign.

He had not. And the beating had continued.

When they left him, he had checked himself. Bruises. But no broken bones. Nothing lasting, nothing that could implicate them.

I can stand this, he had thought.

Next time they used their canes again to rain blows on his back, on his shoulders, his ribs, his legs, the soles of his feet, his face. Aiming for the old bruises. Heaping new pain on top of old pain. Sign . . . sign these papers.

He had gritted his teeth and not signed.

Then they surrounded him and kept beating him with their canes, the rhythm of the blows building up to a frenzy while he cowered on all fours.

Aiming for his back. His legs. His face.

And then the black bubbles burst before his eyes and the abyss rose up to meet him . . .

Night . . .

A gap in time . . .

He opened his eyes and saw them looking down at him.

'Leave him. He can't sign anything now.'

Next morning his urine had a cloudy look, with dark streaks. And clots of blood.

The days after that were a blur. He remembered the thick wooden log, and how they had stripped him and held him down. And pressed down the sides of the log with all their weight as they rolled it over his thighs, back and forth, back and forth. Then they turned him over face down and rolled the log over the backs of his thighs, pressing down hard on the bulge of his hamstrings.

Amma, he remembered, winking out into a distant memory. Amma had a havang-dasta, with a heavy wooden pestle, and she would use it to pound pieces of meat. She would flatten and break down the springy deep-red muscle fibres, and slowly they would be reduced to a sticky paste. And she would use the same dasta to crack the large femur bone in a leg of raw mutton. To release the juices in the marrow.

A red-hot jolt of pain yanked him back to the present. He held his breath, waited for it to subside.

He had expected them to break his bones. But they didn't. When he had looked at his legs the next day he found that they were swollen and covered with red bruises. Traces of purple, blue, green and a jaundiced yellow covered his arms, calves and sides, the bruises from earlier beatings. He remembered staring in fascination at the vivid splashes of colour and touched his cheek and swollen eyelid, knowing that his face looked the same.

Sign, they had said. Or we will go and get the signatures from your mother.

By then he understood it was about a confession. They were going to write a confession on that paper. If he signed the blank paper they were going to put him in jail forever. He had not signed.

He remembered the look on Amma's face just before she had fainted. He had never seen her go to pieces like that before. He knew she could not handle another visit from them. After that blow on her head during the riots, something had changed. She would crack up completely.

The days began to roll together into one, from sleepless nights to long, long spells of just lying there naked and in a stupor on the hard stone floor, unable to stand or even sit up. Waiting. Waiting for more pain to come.

The roller, again, on top of the old bruises. Again and again. While the whole world shrank to just him and his pain.

It was no point screaming, he found. That only made it hurt more. He began to hold his breath when they pressed the hardest, letting the build-up of stale air in his lungs block the pain. A little bit. Sobbing quietly as he exhaled, enough to take in just a tiny sip of fresh air.

How long could he put up with this?

And then yesterday they had taken him and tied him to a frame with his legs apart. And brought an auto rickshaw battery and some wires. Then they attached one wire to his thigh and the other to his left testicle.

For the first time he could feel a sexual excitement in them. They were tense, giggling in anticipation.

'Ab ki baar tu upar jayega!'

He had heard those words before. Somewhere.

And then the blinding pain shot through his groin and he blacked out.

There was dark water everywhere, and he was fighting his way to the surface. His legs kicked and kicked, he couldn't stop them. Air . . . He needed to breathe . . .

He opened his eyes. He was alone again. They had untied him. He moved his hand, slowly, touched his crotch. It was wet. The electrical current had forced him to urinate.

His hand moved and found another point of pain. On his thigh. The exit burn. The place from where the current had left his body.

Then his hand slid back onto the ground, limp, heavy. He was tired. Too tired to move. Gravity has grown, he thought.

He closed his eyes. When he opened them again, he had a sense that time had passed. He lay there alone with the pain and wondered if they had damaged him permanently this time.

Why was he fighting them?

If he signed, they would put him in jail. If he did not sign, he was absolutely certain now, he was going to die. He would simply vanish with without a trace.

He closed his eyes again. In his pocket, a cell phone rang. Megh. She was in a rick and it was night and she was afraid. He tried to tell her that he was in a grave in Shah Alam cemetery, but his lips would not move. He has made a wrong turn. He . . .? Yes, you know him. He has a face like a field rat.

He woke up with his heart pounding. Turned his head and

looked around the dim shuttered room. He was alone. He was alive . . .

And then the pain returned.

Two days later, they came again.

'Sorry, boss! Thodisi galti ho gayi! Slight mistake. You went to sleep and missed the fun. This time you will stay awake . . . enjoy!'

They took him and strapped him again to the frame so that his legs could not move. Turned and brought the wires. He stared in horror. His heart began to pound.

Then the pain screamed through him. He felt his eyes roll inside his head. His body shook and convulsed.

They stood back and considered him. Waited for him to be still. Then they picked up the wires again . . .

'No!' he burst out. 'Please! No more!'

They paused.

'I . . .'

'You will sign? No more nasha?'

'I will sign . . .'

They brought pages of legal size notepaper and gave him a pen.

'Where?'

'Doesn't matter. But left side is best.'

He signed. 'Now you will take me before the magistrate?'

'Not so fast! You still have some days here with us.'

But the light in their eyes was different. He allowed himself to relax. A part of the nightmare was over.

Water to bathe . . . Clothes again . . .

A few days later, when his face was clear of bruises, they

took him to a brightly lit room. A tall young man a bit older than him was sitting on the floor with electrical wires and mechanics' tools all around him.

They put him to sit there next to him.

The tall man leant forward and without looking at him whispered: 'Anees.'

'Adil.'

Silence.

The men brought a camera into the room and set it up on a tripod.

He looked again at the items around him. A glass bottle full of crystals. Shards of aluminium. A small circuit board. A few other things he didn't recognize. Wires.

Steel tiffin boxes.

'Oh *shit* . . .!'

'What?'

'It's about those bomb blasts last year!'

They positioned the two of them with all the bomb-making material in full view.

Click.

Like that night at Law Garden when he had been fixing that extension board.

'They clicked you too?'

'In my shop.'

They brought in more boys and posed them with the bomb material.

Click.

Then a closer shot of aluminium shards in the tiffin box. Look up!

Click.

A few days passed and then they took six of them and herded them into a vehicle for the ride into Ahmedabad. To be produced in front of the magistrate.

'Don't forget. We still have you for a few days in the lock-up before they put you in Sabarmati jail. So don't get any ideas.'

Adil and Anees waited their turn to approach the magistrate and sign their confessions.

'What about these four chargesheets? Where are the confessions?'

'The boys are absconding. Not yet found.'

'How many here?'

'Six.'

'Let us start then.'

The first boy was handed his confession. 'But I can't read this! I don't even know Gujarati!'

'It is what you only have said. Just sign!'

'No! I don't know what it says!'

The magistrate frowned. Looked up. 'You have not prepared him properly.'

They took him away.

'Now he is going to die,' Anees whispered.

Adil's turn came.

'Please read it.'

He skipped over the preamble, his personal details. Reached the part about the elaborate conspiracy he and twenty-one other boys were involved in: to make bombs and deploy them in different parts of the city. For which he was now 'atoning'.

He had already signed the pages on the back. He looked up at the magistrate.

The magistrate looked back at him with cold suspicion.

He took the pen and signed again.

All of a sudden, the air in the room felt lighter. He filled his lungs, enjoyed his first breath of air since the morning.

The magistrate gave a grim smile and remanded him into judicial custody with immediate effect.

His time in Bungalow 16 was over.

22

He was first frisked to make sure he was not carrying a cell phone or any other prohibited item, and then they took him to the after-barrack of the Sabarmati jail, where he spent the first night.

The next morning, he was taken to meet the jailer, where he was briefed about the norms of the jail. They took his photo and his thumb impression and issued him a History Ticket, which listed his name, his undertrial status, his prisoner number and the section of the Indian Penal Code under which he was being booked.

There seemed to be only Muslim prisoners in the barrack he and Anees were allotted. All of them were male and most were young. As undertrials, they did not have a prison uniform, but most of them had opted to wear izaar, the white Muslim-style shin-length pajamas and white kurtas. Many of them even wore skullcaps.

Adil had the eerie feeling of having been enrolled in an Islamic seminary.

'This way is easier for Ramzaan meal timings. And namaaz,' a voice behind him piped up in English. Adil turned and saw a short man with an earnest pair of eyes fixed on him. 'And barrack with same yard as us is also Muslim barrack.' A pause. 'Myself Rasheed. We will look after you, brother, not to worry.'

At first his mind rebelled against the thought of regular namaaz. Images of clear skies still played inside his head, along with the new notion that religion made you un-free. But then he looked around him and saw that he was already in captivity because of religion, and likely to stay that way for a good long while. Megh and her dreams of freedom were far away.

The day to day running of the Sabarmati jail was done by the prisoners themselves. Convicted prisoners were employed as wardens and watchmen, and they were identifiable by the stripes on their uniform caps. Each barrack had one warden and one watchman.

'This is now five-star jail,' crowed Rasheed, who had been an undertrial there for over a year. 'Whole jail is managed by prisoner who is even ex-IIM!' A convict with an MBA from the Indian Institute of Management.

The mood in the jail was strangely upbeat. Adil wondered if it just seemed that way to him in comparison to the dimness and squalor in the lock-up.

'No,' Rasheed assured him. 'We have got new superintendent. Only few months back. That is real reason.' He looked over his shoulder. 'But he is different kind. Coming and talking to us.' He shook his head. 'They will shift him, I think.'

And so Adil fell in with the new routine. The day would

start at 6 a.m. sharp, when the barracks were opened and the inmates were sent out into the yard that they shared with the other Muslim barrack. Then, at 6.15, they got morning chai.

'Exactly 20 ml,' Rasheed told him. 'More than that, you must pay.'

The payment would be in jail coupons. The jail had its own currency, with each inmate being given up to 800 jail coupons per month. They could spend these to buy items from the jail canteen, which was also run by convicted prisoners.

At 9.30 they had their lunch. The kitchen too was run by convicted prisoners, who were housed in a separate barrack with different timings to allow for preparation time and clean up. But, for the others, noon was the time to return to barracks. Then at 3 p.m., the barracks would reopen, and the inmates would get tea. And dinner came some time between 4.30 and 5 in the evening.

'Four chapattis, 100 ml dal, one scoop sabzi,' Rasheed recited as orientation. 'Means: one scoop vegetables. And rice. After 6 p.m., go back to barrack, jail closed. No food after that: only canteen.'

Adil and Anees watched him move on after he had completed his spiel.

He turned to Anees, slipped back into Gujarati. 'You got all of that?'

'Yes.'

'But why is he talking to me in English?'

'Because you are educated, Adil-bhai. And the youngest in the group. He is trying to bond with you. That is good: it means he is going to look out for you.'

At the far end of the yard, three older bearded men with the look of mafiosi were watching them intently.

'Come, Adil-bhai,' Anees whispered. 'Better we go and make contact before they send for us.'

He followed Anees across the yard.

'I am Anees,' Adil heard him tell the dons. 'And Adil is . . . like my younger brother. We are POTA . . .'

'Yes, we know,' the oldest don said gravely.

'And we heard you gave them trouble in the lock-up,' another don added.

Anees shrugged. 'At that time I didn't care.'

'The point is, don't worry about anything. For them you are a terrorist. So for us you are a hero.'

Anees gave them an extravagant salaam and they made their way back to their corner of the yard.

'You let him think we really did it,' Adil said. 'Not a good idea, Anees. This is going to get back to the jail staff.'

'I said nothing,' Anees replied, unperturbed. 'But we had to get them off our backs. You are educated, Adil, so you don't know.' He paused, searching for the right words. 'This place is full of gang activity. You have to be careful, and not get into any fights . . .'

'I don't think I ever got into a fight in my whole life!'

'No, listen,' Anees went on seriously. 'This is a jail. Some of these men will keep after you and try to get you to react. Or they will bully.' He shook his head. 'You have to avoid, Adil. If *they* see you in a fight,' he cast his glance up, 'they will try to file another case against you. Or they will decide they are going to keep you.' He shrugged. 'They will just arrest you again even if you get acquitted. If someone troubles you, just tell *me*.'

'And then what will you do? Take my side and fight for me?' Adil shook his head. 'No, Anees. I don't want you to put yourself in this kind of trouble. Don't try to be a hero. It will go against you.'

Anees hesitated. 'Adil, you don't know, but I signed two confessions, not just one. So I am already chargesheeted in two cases. And they have got signatures from my father, and maybe from other witnesses.' He shrugged. 'So I am not getting out of this jail except by a miracle.'

'But . . .'

'Even if the judge decides to acquit me in this case, they have another case they can use to keep me here.'

'But *why*?'

Anees smiled grimly. 'In the lock up . . .'

'Bungalow 16 . . .'

'Yes. Well, I had decided that I was finished anyway. So something tripped, inside my brain. I started to see the whole thing as a game. I got bugged with them. Safe and smug, just doing it as a job.' He paused. 'So while they tortured me, I used to taunt them. Dare them to do more. You know?'

'No, Anees, I *don't* know.' Adil shuddered. Do *more*?

'And they would,' he went on coolly. 'But after some time, I think even they got confused. In the end they decided that I was crazy. Like one of those people who enjoy that kind of thing.'

'Then why did you sign?'

'Then they went and arrested my father.'

Just as they were always saying they would go after Amma.

'And, well, the old man has a bad heart. And asthma. And they would come and tell me what they were doing to him . . .' He broke off.

'And in the end you signed,' Adil finished the sentence for him.

'Yes. I signed. They made me sign enough of those long pages for *two* confessions. They are not going to let me go. Not a hope! And I don't care: it was worth it. But *you* might get out.' He gave Adil a long meaningful look. 'Why do you want to spoil that chance, brother?'

Adil looked around the yard. There were at least a hundred Muslim boys milling around them, all of them undertrials. Just in this yard.

'You know,' Adil ventured, 'the whole thing is so silly. I mean: like setting off firecrackers, more to get attention than to really do any damage.' He paused, looked up at Anees. 'If anyone really wanted to take badla for the riots, they knew who they had to get. It wasn't so difficult.'

Anees nodded. 'I was also wondering why we did not see a more serious response.'

'I have a theory.'

Anees cocked his head, waited.

'People only get up and do something like that if . . . they feel *safe* doing it.'

'Or if they are so desperate that they don't care,' Anees added. 'Like in Kashmir.'

'Yes. But this is not like Kashmir. There they are the majority. We are not even a proper minority in this state! We are just *one* of . . . seven–eight Muslim groups living here. And we are *not* safe. People in our localities are getting killed the minute anything violent happens that they want to blame on us. They are kept like hostages.' He paused, finding his way. 'So most of us . . . like me, like you, kept our heads down and tried to merge. Put the whole thing behind us.' He paused again. Hesitated. 'Started looking out, and even doubting some of the things we were brought up to believe.'

'You did?'

'I am trying to understand what was going on in my mind.'

'We backed off because someone up there decided to change the game,' Anees declared, rolling his eyes upward. 'We did not even have space to think for ourselves. We were just trying to stay alive in the jaws of death.' He shrugged. 'And, for a time, we could.'

Adil nodded. 'We are not dead. But . . . they have us. The young men. And at the slightest excuse they will keep us here forever.'

'*That* is what I was talking about, brother. *My* plan is that you should go free.'

After that, Anees followed him like a shadow. The weeks went by and Adil found himself falling in line and joining the others in namaaz.

Time-pass, he told himself at first. I need a shape to the day, a sense of time. And connection. Without that, I will truly cease to exist.

But as the months went by, he began to value the routine of namaaz, and the sense of peace it brought to his life. When he was alone with his thoughts he would still recall the light in

Megha's eyes as they had sat on the grass at Law Garden drinking their chai, when she had told him that she was an atheist. But as he joined the others in namaaz, he began to get the strange feeling that he was doing something that would make him a better person. The things that had made him feel good about himself before – his work, his plans for college, his Megh – all belonged to another life. He now had to search for something within himself that could see him through this time in jail.

'It's funny, but namaaz seems to be the only thing I do these days that leaves me feeling worthwhile,' he confided to Anees.

Anees nodded. 'I used to look at the young ones going for namaaz every Friday. So many of them were out of work.' He paused. 'They even looked . . . smaller, you know? Not happy. But I had to mind my shop. So I mostly didn't go. But now . . .'

'I know.'

One morning he received a mulaqaat slip. Two people had come to meet him. His Chacha and Faiza.

At 10 o'clock sharp he was there, waiting in the mulaqaat room.

He saw them come through the doorway. Faiza looked tired, drawn.

'Faizoo,' he began. 'Chacha. How are you? And how is Amma?'

'Bhai,' she began solemnly, 'we had to take Amma back to Surat. The doctor there says she has had a breakdown, but now I think she is getting better. She still says she is not able to remember anything that happened during the riots. But every night she wakes up with a bad dream.' She paused. 'Sorry, Bhai, for not coming much before.'

'A breakdown! But how did you . . .' He looked from her to Chacha.

'I have come back with Chachu. For schooling. We are staying in the house.' She paused. 'But Bhai, it is not like before. People see us and they are afraid, so now they are avoiding us. As if all of us are terrorists all of a sudden.'

'How are *you*, son?' his uncle intervened.

'Chacha, I am all right. Now. But the first few weeks were bad. I was in the police lock-up.' He paused. 'They beat me and made me sign a confession. That I was in the group that did the bombings last year.' He gave them an anguished look. 'If I did not sign, I knew I was going to die. So I signed.'

'Oh, Bhai,' Faiza cried suddenly, 'why did you come home that night? Why didn't you run away like I told you? Then this would not have happened!'

'Then they would have arrested Amma in my place,' he corrected her firmly. 'Some of the boys here only came and surrendered when they found that their fathers and brothers had been taken away as hostages. And some of the old men are still with the police. No, Faizoo,' he shook his head. 'This is better.'

'But when they release you, we will go from here, na, Bhai? You promise?'

'*If* they release me, you mean.'

'You have to promise.'

'Okay,' he smiled. 'Promise.'

'You will need a lawyer,' his uncle cut in. 'With your permission, I will start to look.'

'Yes,' Adil agreed. 'We will all need lawyers, maybe the same lawyer. It is the same case we are all involved in.'

'Then you have to get their families' contacts for me. Next mulaqaat I will take their names and phone numbers from you.'

Back in the barrack, Adil discussed with Anees what his uncle wanted.

'Leave it to me,' Anees decided. 'I will talk to them and get all the contacts. It is a good idea. And it is time to begin.'

But it was a slow start. Four of the boys opted out and got their own lawyers. And the first lawyers Adil's group got did not work out. Winter came and went, and the next summer too. And then when the city of Ahmedabad was getting ready for a festival that celebrated the defeat of a demon with ten heads, Adil's uncle came with the news that he had found a group of lawyers that was excited about the case, a group that felt there was a good chance that they would be able to get the boys released.

One day shortly after that, a young lawyer by the name of Apoorva-bhai came to the jail for mulaqaat. Asking all the right questions. Looking ready to go the full distance with them. And he talked of a whole legal team that was gearing up for a showdown with the forces that had abducted them and kept them in confinement.

It was just a hope. Just a faint glimpse of a possibility. But on that day, as he walked back to the barrack, Adil had a sense that something had begun.

Rasheed walked past him on his way to the yard. He stopped and sniffed the air and smiled at Adil. 'Now is coming good weather . . .'

23

'Ridiculous!' She looked up from the pile of papers, fuming.

'What, Ma'am?' the office assistant asked nervously.

'*How* can I do a story on boys who have disappeared if I don't get to see anything about them anywhere? What kind of reports have you people been filing? Everything about the cops and the courts, but nothing about the boys . . .'

'Sorry, Ma'am.'

'I want a list of names. For a start. Where can I get it?'

One of the senior reporters heard the commotion and ambled by. 'What is it, Megha?'

'Is there any place in Ahmedabad that has been keeping track of this case? Where I can find some information about the *boys*?'

'Just a minute,' he whipped out his cell phone and punched a few buttons. Wrote down some names and a phone number and gave it to her. 'Here. This is an NGO that works on human rights issues. They have been keeping cuttings from all the newspapers on things like this. So they might have something . . .' He nodded. 'Give them a call: the man who runs it is an old priest. Just tell him I gave you his number.'

She caught a rick and headed for Drive-In Road, and started looking for the landmarks the old priest had given her. Where . . .?

'Stop!' she told the driver. 'I think we left it behind.'

She called the NGO's number again.

'Turn back . . .' She started looking along the pavement.

A jolly old man waved out to her and smiled.

'Bas!' She paid the driver and got down.

'Welcome,' he said, ushering her into the building. He pointed to a large open room on their left. 'That is where we keep the newspaper cuttings. But we have more boxes upstairs.'

He took her into his own office and they sat down. First chai. 'Now how can I help?'

'Well,' she began, 'I'm doing research for a documentary about the bomb blasts in 2002. I want to focus on the boys who have been arrested. But the reports I see only talk about the police, or about the courts. Or the damage.' She shrugged. 'Just two or three names keep coming up in a few reports. I was hoping I could get the full list of the boys from you.'

'Do you read Gujarati?'

'No, sorry!'

'Well, the most detailed reports on this are in the Gujarati press. But I can ask my staff to get out what we have in English for you.'

'Could I have a look at the Gujarati clippings too?' she ventured timidly. 'And would they be able to translate them for me? I mean, verbally.'

'Why not?' He got up and bustled into the room outside.

Half an hour later she was sitting at a desk with a pile of

Gujarati news clippings in front of her. A young researcher sat opposite her scanning through them one by one looking for names.

'Here!' she said at last. 'This one has a list.'

'Can you read it to me?'

The girl nodded and started to rattle off the boys' names. Megha decided she would ask for a Xerox copy of the article.

'. . . Adil Ansari . . .'

'Wait!' Megha sat up bolt upright. 'What did you just say?'

'I said: Adil Ansari.'

'Show me!'

She turned the clipping so that Megha could read it, and pointed to the name.

Megha focused her eyes on the tiny unknown letters and tried to find some similarity to the letters that would spell his name in Hindi. And then the two words came through to her like a weak radio signal.

Adil Ansari.

She slumped on the desk. All this time he had been in jail! And she had been cursing him for vanishing out of her life.

She shivered as all the banished memories came rushing back. Like a surge of sweetness.

That afternoon in her room, after she had closed the door . . .

At first he had looked away, unable to meet her open gaze. And she had reached up and turned his face to hers. Seen his eyes burning with love, felt him quiver as her fingers brushed his cheek. Hovering on the brink of the inferno. Touch me again . . .

And she had taken his face in her hands and gone up on tiptoe, and kissed him slowly and lovingly.

Then he had reached out and pulled her close, holding her against him with all his trembling might until she felt herself melting inside. Don't stop . . .

She looked around the little library, drew a deep shuddering breath.

She had woken up the next morning and felt his arms around her, his warm breath on her shoulder. As she turned, he had opened his eyes and looked at her with wonder. Reached out and touched her face to be sure it was not a dream. All through the day, he never left her thoughts: the little SMSes he kept sending, telling her that she was there in everything he saw, every shot he framed. His voice over the cell phone, strong and urgent, telling her he couldn't wait till they were together again.

Then that evening he had left her to go home for the night – and disappeared. Vanished off the face of the Earth.

She had woken up alone with a strange uneasy feeling. She tried to call him. But all she got was a recorded response in Gujarati that his number was unavailable. And she realized that she did not even know where he lived. Then she remembered the studio where he worked, and decided to go and see if there was any news of him there.

The others there who worked with him had averted their eyes when they saw her, and mumbled that they did not know where he was. They insisted that that they knew nothing. He was *gone*. And they did not want to talk about him.

In the weeks after his disappearance, she tried to bury her memories and put it all down to an adventure. A failed adventure, as much for him as it had been for her. He must have . . . lost his nerve. And not been able to face her and tell her that he couldn't go on with the relationship.

But where was he? Shouldn't she have run into him on a shoot?

She was ready for the I-told-you-so looks she got. It didn't work out, she would shrug off all their questions. It happens. I'm cool.

Now she wanted to kick herself. She had been so busy telling herself that he was just like her that she had never stopped to think that, as a Muslim, he lived in a dangerous town. Why hadn't it even crossed her mind that he could be in trouble? I'm no better than . . .

'Are you all right, Ma'am?'

She looked up in surprise. 'Yes,' she breathed. 'I have to find him!'

'The lawyers on the case come down from Delhi for the court appearances,' the old priest told her when she stumbled back into his office and asked for the name of his lawyer. 'But one of them lives in Ahmedabad.' He paused and flipped through a notebook, picked up a pencil and wrote down a name and a number. 'Here. His name is Apoorva-bhai. Give him a call, and tell him that I gave you his number.' He paused and thought for a moment, changed his mind: 'No. I'll call him and put you on. If he sees an unknown number calling, he might not pick up.'

Apoorva-bhai said he would be free to meet her at his home the next morning. She took down the directions, picked up a copy of the list and thanked the old priest with all her heart.

Next morning, she climbed the steps to Apoorva-bhai's flat, rang the doorbell and was shown into his study. She sat looking at the old computer and the cluttered desk while he went off to make chai for them. She noted that he had already printed out a list of the boys for her. Names, ages and their home addresses.

He came in with the chai, took his place across the desk from her and handed her the list.

Adil Ansari. Age eighteen at the time of arrest. Resident of Jamalpur.

His sister had said that they were coming from their home in Jamalpur that day. And that it had just been broken into and vandalized.

'I think it's him,' she decided.

'Adil Ansari . . .' he mused. 'I remember him. The youngest suspect. But are you sure? I mean: why would they have wanted to pick up someone like your friend? They were not looking for people like cameramen. The boys they picked up were mostly mechanics, or electricians. Things like that. Boys who knew how to use tools. The sort of boys who could, arguably, have made the bombs.'

She thought back to that night at Law Garden. A memory flickered before her of the producer handing him an extension board. Which he had opened up easily and was fixing when someone came and took some pictures of him, with a flash.

She also remembered the look of horror on his face afterwards. She had had to call him and pretend that they were ready to start.

'Someone came and took pictures of him fixing an extension

board. At Law Garden. During a shoot. The same day the Minister was killed.'

Apoorva-bhai nodded slowly, took a long look out the window. A tall dusty tree gave a dappled view of the people walking on the road outside.

'You can go for mulaqaat, you know.'

'Mulaqaat? Isn't that Urdu for meeting?'

'Yes. Mulaqaat means going to meet a prisoner in jail.'

'How do I do that?'

'You need to go there and give your name. Then he will be informed so that he will be there to meet you.'

'As easy as that?'

'Yes. Mulaqaat is at 10 a.m. and 4 p.m. You can give in your name and fix it for tomorrow morning.'

She woke up next morning wondering if it had all been a dream.

No, she remembered. This morning she was going to see her Adil again!

On impulse, she decided not to wear her jeans, but to dress in Indian clothes. She checked her suitcase and saw that she had also packed a teal-coloured dupatta. She picked it up and remembered the look on Adil's face when she had stepped out of the car that day with her head covered by the peach dupatta. His eyes had widened, and then taken on a dreamy look.

That first night in her room, she had remembered that look and asked him, just before they fell asleep, if he didn't like her better with her dupatta on.

And he had laughed, wrapped his arms around her and told

her that he loved her every which way. But that when a man saw the woman he loved with her head covered, she became magically beautiful, and his alone.

She pulled the dupatta carefully over her head, fluffing it out to frame her face better, draping the folds over from behind to cover her ears. Then she flipped one end under her chin and across the opposite shoulder, letting it hang down her back.

And she went out to find a rick that would take her to Sabarmati jail.

24

Adil woke up to the light of a day that was already searingly hot. The sun had barely risen, but the sky was already a bleached-out white.

He heard Rasheed warbling away in his cracked besura voice an old, old song that seemed to spill straight out of last night's dream.

Megh . . .

Allah megh de, chhaya de, pani de-de,
Allah megh de.

Not a chance, brother, he thought, as he got up to follow the others out into the yard for morning chai. Not a cloud in the sky. And my Megh must be far away.

A mulaqaat slip: someone by the name of M. Rai to see him.

He finished his chai and fetched his bucket, joined the queue for the tiny bath cubicles at the far end of the yard along the wall. His turn came, and he put down his bucket, hung up his threadbare towel and opened the tap. Waited for his bucket to fill up.

M. Rai?

Must be a new lawyer on the team, he decided.

At 10 o'clock sharp he was standing behind the grille in the mulaqaat room.

She came through the door and stood a moment in the distance, panning her gaze to locate him. Her face was framed in a deep ferozi blue dupatta that made her eyes look like glowing honey.

Megh . . .

Hain khwaab mein hanooz jo jaage hain khwaab se. Those who wake up from a dream are still deep inside that dream. Ghalib's words rang in his head.

He held his breath. This isn't real!

'Adil!' she cried, hurrying over to his window.

He stood and stared at her.

'You've grown a beard,' she said softly.

His hand went to his chin, a reflex. 'How did you find me, Megh?'

'I came to Ahmedabad to do some research for a film. A documentary on the boys who have disappeared in "Shining Gujarat". Yesterday someone was reading me a list of the names. And I got the shock of my life!'

'A film?' He smiled and shook his head. 'Nooooo, Megh! You were going to make a film with some other cameraman?'

She opened her mouth to protest. Then she smiled back at him, the glow on her face fading up to the colour temperature of outdoor sunlight.

'You know the word humsafar?' he asked gently.

She nodded. 'Someone who makes the same journey as you.'

'Or two people who make the same journey. Like you and me. First we meet in the Old City, in the riots. Then we land up at the same news shoot at Law Garden, on the same side of the camera. And now you, of all people, are here to make a film on the lost boys in Ahmedabad!'

'We always seem to find each other when the world is coming to an end,' she said wonderingly. 'I think . . . when we are not together . . . it's like the whole world goes wrong.'

'Megh,' he broke in desperately, 'I've missed you. So bad. You can't even imagine.' His eyes held hers. 'There hasn't been a single day that I haven't thought of you.'

A heartbeat of silence.

'I was *so* mad at you,' she murmured. 'I thought you had run off. I even wondered if you had had an . . . arranged marriage.'

'A *what?*' He stared at her again, shook his head. 'I can't get you out of my mind for even a minute and I'm going to go and have an arranged marriage with someone else? Are you crazy?'

'Sorry . . .' she breathed.

'It's okay,' he smiled. 'You're here, so the whole world is alive again.'

She remembered what she had come to say. 'I went and met your lawyer yesterday,' she said. 'I got the feeling that you were one of the ones they had some hope for. Of getting you released.' A pause. 'But Adil, they are not going to make it easy for you.' Her eyes took in the whole jail in a sweeping glance.

'I know. They haven't released a single POTA prisoner.'

'So you have to keep off their radar. Keep such a low profile that you are almost invisible. They should have no reason to *want* to keep you.'

He shook his head. 'It is not like that, Megh. This is not a normal situation. They didn't arrest us because they thought we had actually done something wrong. They rounded us up under POTA because they needed to show suspects. To cover up what they did to the minister.' He frowned. 'What I mean is: I don't think it really matters how I behave. They are going to keep me here.'

'Adil!' she protested. 'You can't give up like this . . .'

'I am trying to be realistic, Megh. I am in here for . . .'

'Whatever! But I am going to plan as though you are getting out.'

He shrugged. 'A friend of mine told me the same thing. Anees. He said that *his* plan is that I must go free. Since he doesn't think *he* will . . .' He turned his head and tried to locate Anees, who had also come for mulaqaat with his parents.

She nodded sadly. 'I remember the name. He is charge-sheeted in two cases.' She took a deep breath, changed the subject. 'I'm not in Ahmedabad these days, Adil. I've shifted back to Delhi for my diploma project. So I can only come and see you when I am here. But I *will* be coming to Ahmedabad, so I *will* keep coming to see you.'

'You can write, too.'

'Yes. I will. But what I wanted to ask was: is there anything *you* want me to do for you? Get you anything? Meet anyone?'

He was about to say no when a thought struck him. 'Well, there is *one* thing you could do for me. I don't know how to ask this . . .'

'Just ask!'

'Amma . . . and Faiza. They are alone. More alone that ever before. Even the neighbours are avoiding them.' He paused. 'They are all scared. Everyone there is scared. I don't really blame them.'

'Do you want me to go and see them? To keep in touch with them?'

'Do you think you could? Amma is not well. The night they came and arrested me, she had a sort of breakdown. And something of that day came back, some memory in the form of nightmares.' He took a breath. 'She had partial amnesia after she was hit on the head. But now it looks like she was actually hurt worse than that.'

'Oh no!'

'Faiza says she wants us to leave Ahmedabad. When I am released. *If* I am released. I think the only thing keeping them here now is me.'

Her eyes flashed a moment. 'Then we'll call that Plan A. Your job is to get out of this place, and then all of you leave Ahmedabad.' She held his gaze intently. 'I'm sorry to put this burden on you, Adil. But for your mother's sake, you have to do everything you can so that they have no objection to releasing you.'

'Megh . . .'

'Do you have a better idea?'

'No,' he conceded. 'And if that doesn't work?'

Silence. Her eyes narrowed at once, darkened to a deep bottle green. 'Well, as they say: there is no Plan B. Not from my side. When you are released from this jail, you can't stay in Ahmedabad. And there is no reason to, now. There is nothing left for you here.'

'There isn't,' he mused. 'And if we shift, we might as well leave Gujarat.' He paused, remembered Dilnawaz, and his first shoot on Dumas Beach in Surat. 'Once before I had a chance to leave, before all this happened. And I didn't take it.' He shook his head. 'I was only thinking of my Boards. And then I got excited about the chance to be a cameraman.'

'Don't look back, Adil. It's a waste of time.'

He smiled ruefully. 'I have lots of time.'

'Well, I'll go and see your Mom and Faiza this evening. They'll probably be home.' She looked up into his eyes, her expression softening as she remembered. 'Adil . . .'

He caught his breath as images from last night's dream streaked across his mind. He resisted the urge to turn away in embarrassment.

'Megh . . .' he began hoarsely. 'Your . . . film? You said you were going to make a film about us?'

She stared at him, nonplussed for a moment. 'My film? Yes. But I don't know . . . I mean, how do I get visuals? And there is so little information . . .'

'No,' he insisted. 'There's lots of information. And visuals. Just ask me. I can tell you everything.' He held her gaze easily now. 'You should make it, Megh. Really.'

'I can't bring a camera in here . . .'

'You don't have to. You can draw. Like you used to. Or mock up the things I tell you about. High-contrast black-and-white shots. Stills.'

'Yes,' she breathed. 'We could start with the night we were

covering the minister's assassination. The flash and the shots they took of you at Law Garden. Fixing the extension board . . .'

Adil ambled back to the yard after mulaqaat in a bright crystalline cocoon of dreams, replaying his memories of every smile, every expression, everything she had said. I feel like a cameraman again, he thought. More than a cameraman. My brain is working now . . .

'Hey!' Anees's voice broke into his reverie. 'Who was *that*?'

'Oh!' Adil came back down to Earth. 'She is . . . she is someone I used to work with . . .' he said cryptically, throwing another veil over her head. His alone.

'You found girls like that at . . . work?' Anees raised an eyebrow.

'Yes . . .'

'Adil-bhai,' Anees shot back, 'mujhe to aisi naukri dilwa do!'

Adil looked back at him, a new idea taking shape in his mind. 'She is making a film about what happened to us. She wants me to help her. You know, tell her details, things like that. And maybe she should talk to you too.' He cocked his head. 'So Anees-bhai, I think you have got your job!'

They walked out into the yard. A few wisps of cloud had obscured the worst of the sun's glare.

Adil sat down in the timeless light and let the events and images of the last two and a half years return, float around freely in his mind and string themselves into a script.

25

She took a rick to Jamalpur Darwaza. Got down, and looked around to find her bearings. She followed Adil's directions to the ground floor flat where they lived, and knocked softly on the door.

Silence. Then the sound of bare feet, and the voice of a young girl behind the locked door. 'Who is it?'

'Faiza.' She hesitated. 'It's . . . Megha.'

The door opened a crack and a face she remembered peeked out cautiously from behind a pair of glasses. 'It's *you!*' she exclaimed. 'But how . . .?'

'Adil gave me your address,' she said softly. 'I am just coming from mulaqaat with him. Are you busy? I can come back later.'

'No, Megha-ben! *Please* come!' The door opened fully and she was led into a small living room. Adil's mother looked up as she entered. 'Amma! This is Megha-ben. We met her on the day the riots started. In the old city.'

Amma smiled. 'You are a friend of Adil's?'

She nodded.

'Megha-ben!' Faiza burst out. 'How do you know Bhai? You were only talking to me!'

'I got to know him later. I was helping out in the same news team where he was doing the camera. Then one morning . . . he just disappeared. And no one in the studio would tell me what had happened. Like it was . . . some sort of secret.' She sat down hesitantly on the divan next to his mother. 'I didn't even know where he lived, or I would have come much before, Auntie.' She paused. 'Then I had to come back to Ahmedabad to do some research for a film, and the day before yesterday I was looking through old newspapers and I saw a list of names of boys who had been arrested . . .' she broke off. 'His lawyer told me about mulaqaat, so I went to see him today.'

'And he is well?'

'Yes. But he is worried about you.'

Amma shifted her weight, turned to face Megha. 'I am much better now. In fact, I have joined work again, part-time. I am a teacher.'

'I know. He told me you are an Urdu teacher.'

She nodded. Then she looked up abruptly. 'Faiza! Bring my purse!' She turned to Megha. 'You will stay and have khana with us?'

'I don't want you to go and cook anything now. I just wanted to meet you.'

'Arrey, I am not going to cook. Faiza will get something from the market.' Her eyes clouded a moment. 'I would have *liked* to make something for you, but these days I have not been doing too much. I don't know why.'

'What do you want me to get, Amma?'

'A biryani?' She turned and gave Megha a searching look. 'You would eat non-veg?'

'Of course, Auntie! I used to come to the dhabas here for biryani when I was a student!'

Amma handed some money to Faiza, who went and got a metal bowl from the kitchen.

'I can go with you,' Megha began to get up.

'No. You stay with me. I will go and make some chai for us. It's all right,' she shook her head. 'You sit. I will just come.'

Megha looked around the room, with its bookcases full of old books in Urdu. She could recognize the names of a few poets. Then she looked down at the open book that Adil's mother had been reading. Poems by Amir Khusro. She remembered that his poetry was so old that some of his poems were half in Urdu, and half in Persian. He had been writing back in the thirteenth century when the language itself was just being born!

She looked down at a couplet, tried to read it. Frowned.

'Oh! That one is in Persian.' Amma came back into the room with their chai.

'This . . . is what you are teaching the children? In school?'

'No-no,' she sat down next to Megha, picked up the book. 'But I just wanted to look at this one again. I was feeling . . .' she shrugged, 'alone, all of a sudden.'

Megha nodded. 'It sounds so . . . desolate! I just wish I could understand it properly . . . Well, I see one word that I can understand. Judaa.'

'That is the most important word. Being separated. That is why it is repeated so many times. This ghazal is about being separated from someone you love.' She pointed to another word, looked up at Megha.

'Yaar? Friend?'

She nodded. 'Or beloved.' She pointed again. 'And this one?'

'Vidaa? Saying goodbye?'

'Yes: the moment of separation.'

Megha looked again at the text, tried to decipher another word. 'And . . . abr?'

'Oh, that is a Persian word. It means cloud.' She cleared her throat softly, and sat up to translate into modern-day Urdu:

'The cloud weeps as my beloved and I stand saying farewell,
Me, weeping alone, the cloud far away, my beloved far away.'

Silence. Megha felt the sting of tears in her eyes.

'That is what Adil calls me,' she ventured shyly. 'Megh. Cloud . . .'

Adil's mother looked up in surprise. Then she reached out and put her arms around Megha, hugged her tight. 'I am such a fool,' she murmured. 'So wrapped up in my own suffering that I just couldn't see. Of *course* you must be weeping too. Now I understand . . .'

A pause. A bright stillness. Then . . . something stirred. One tiny spark, setting off an archipelago of tinkling reflections, all echoing back to banish the gloom.

'It's like the whole room is full of light!' Megha burst out.

And Amma surged to her feet, suddenly energized. 'I always wondered what that line meant,' she exclaimed, heading for a shelf of old poetry books. 'Now at last I know.' She took down one book, found the page she wanted and brought it back and showed it to Megha, who read it aloud.

'*Hayat raaz-e-sukoon pa gayi, ajal thehri,*
Ajal mein thodisi larzish hui, hayat hui.'

'Yes: "Life has found the secret of peace: and that is death;
but if there should be a little tremor in death, life begins."
The first line is easy to grasp. We have been kept apart all this
time, and have survived only by lulling ourselves into the
peace of death. But now,' Amma smiled, 'it is as you said. It is
as if a spell has been broken. And a heart has begun to beat
again in the centre of the universe!'

Megha read the name of the poet. 'Firaq.'

'You have heard of Firaq? He is a modern poet, and his
Urdu would be much easier for you to follow. But he also
writes about these kinds of things. In fact, his name itself
means separation.'

The door opened, and Faiza was back.

'And . . .' Amma continued, opening the book again, 'and,
do you know? During the Freedom Struggle even *he* spent
time in jail!'

26

I parked my car outside India International Centre in Delhi and walked in the main gate, up the drive, past the lotus pond with its croaking frogs, past the porch and doubled back around the hotel reception area heading for the bar. It was 7 o'clock, and a mild early summer night. The sky was still bright.

I opened the door and peered inside. Hardly anyone yet.

Ramya was sitting at a little table against the far wall with a huge hold-all bag on the floor next to her, engrossed in reading some stapled papers. She looked up as I pulled back a chair and sat down opposite her.

'What is it?' I asked. 'Any news?'

'No,' she said. 'Not yet. I called you here because the transcript of your testimony has come. You need to go through it before they hand it over to the judge.' She gave me the stapled pages she had been reading. 'I think there are a few mistakes. Some of it is a bit strange.'

I focused my eyes on the typed transcript and willed it to make sense.

Ramya waved the waiter away and he headed back to the bar. Later.

I read past the introduction, which gave my qualifications and the reference to the other POTA case I had helped with. The bit about the videotape and the unbroken time code. And then the confusion hit. I decided to read that paragraph out loud.

'What Dr Sahai wanted to see was how a scribe like you takes down testimony, what happens to handwriting under pressure, what speed you are able to maintain. What adjustments the speaker giving the testimony has to make to accommodate you.' I looked up.

'That's where I got stuck,' Ramya nodded. 'Who is this "you"? I've never seen anything like this on a transcript before. Can you remember what you said?'

I tried to take myself back into the courtroom in Sabarmati jail. I imagined the judge sitting at the raised platform, her pale skin translucent in the spotlight that singled her out and left the rest of the room in dimness. Just along from her sat an earnest man with thinning hair and a bandh-gala formal jacket, like the kaatib in that Turkish song. He was nodding at me. A scribe . . .

Mr Verma!

A scribe like you!

I had been talking directly to Mr Verma, to bring him into the conversation, since he too was a scribe, like the man who would have taken down the confession. And like Jaafer-bhai. And Anoop.

He had omitted the bit at the beginning where I had specifically asked to be introduced to the Court Recorder, and his response then, giving his name. He had probably not judged it to be relevant to my testimony.

How *could* I have forgotten Mr Verma?

'I was speaking to Mr Verma at the time.'

'Mr Verma?' she frowned.

'The Court Recorder. I told you. I wanted to bring him into the conversation since the whole thing was about the work of scribes. Don't you remember?'

'Maybe. So he is the "you"?'

'Yes. Can I write on the transcript?'

She nodded. 'That's what you're supposed to do. Why I called you here.'

I whipped out the red ballpoint pen I always carried and wrote clearly in print just above the 'you': '(Spoken to Mr H.C. Verma, Court Recorder)'.

'He will edit out his name from the final version and say Court Recorder,' Ramya remarked dryly. 'Just as well.'

Mr Verma was back in my life! I burrowed into the pages to read the rest of his missive.

'No more problems?'

'Nope!' I slowed down deliberately and conjured up in my mind's eye the scene in the courtroom as I read his depiction of it. He had fully understood my line of argument, got all the numbers right and had even managed to include the bit about scribes in Gujarat writing in Modi script, which was faster and more suited to taking down court confessions. I smiled.

'What?'

'Modi script.'

'Yeah. Everyone remembers how you brought in that name.'

I went on to the cross-examination. Read past my opening explanation about what linguistics was about. And then

Mr Verma's account segued neatly into an explanation about my own view about what was meant by nationalism.

I re-read that paragraph. Smooth. Too smooth.

I backtracked to the start of the cross-examination. Gone was the prosecutor's opening remark about his understanding that linguists were people who knew many languages. His allegation that I must be biased since I was doing the work *pro bono*. That I myself must be anti-national. Gone was the little catfight between the prosecutor and me where Ramya and the judge had had to intervene. Mr Verma had decided that none of that was relevant to the case.

But he *had* recorded the final questions from the judge, and my assessment of the actual speed at which the confession statement would have been written: 'Twenty to twenty-two words per minute. Definitely not more than twenty-five.' And my conclusion that there was no way that the confessions could have been obtained in the manner in which the police were claiming.

And then he ended the document with the prosecutor's last question, asking that I specify, from the look of the confessions, exactly how they had been recorded. And my parting shot: 'Dr Sahai requested the prosecutor to use his imagination about the manner in which the confessions might have been obtained, since she felt that he would know the Gujarat police better than she would.'

'I love you, Mr Verma!' I announced with a huge grin.

'What are you on about now?'

'Read it!' I exulted, thrusting the transcript back at her, almost dancing a jig, jumping around in my seat with my hands in the air. The bartender looked up from behind the counter and grinned back at me. 'He has made me look like the most mature and reliable expert witness in the world!'

'Get her a drink,' Ramya said over her shoulder to the bartender.

'A beer,' I ordered. 'Now I'm off duty.' I turned back to Ramya. 'Well? What do you think?'

My beer came in a stemmed glass and I took a sip, watching her over the rim as she read.

'Hmmm,' she said at last, putting the transcript on a chair and turning to give the waiter a meaningful look. 'Okay, Deepi, it's good. Better than I expected. He's saved your ass.'

'My ass was always fine!' I retorted. 'What he has saved is your case!'

She gave me a long look. I felt myself tumble down from the clouds.

'Deepi, I don't want you to get your hopes up. Just remember that there hasn't been a POTA acquittal up to now in Gujarat. Anything can happen. It's out of our hands now.'

'I know,' I said softly. 'But I've seen it all before. I'll survive . . . It's those boys I'm thinking about. I remember how they looked that day in the jail. It took me a few minutes to realize they weren't college students. I had been deposing in English and I think they understood every word I said.'

'I'm not so sure . . .'

'Well, the one I talked to did. Adil. The youngest suspect.' I shook my head. 'I think about him a lot. Funny world we live in: the boys in jail as serial bombers are educated and courteous, while the guardians of the law look and behave like goons.'

Her drink came and she took a sip. The room began to hum. Regulars began to trickle in like goblins coming out of the cracks after sunset. The average age in the bar kept rising. The place was, after all, a club. Members and guests only.

Reality. I sighed, wondering how young Adil would relate to this rude outside world where goons and goblins roamed about freely with all sorts of access, while nice, well-bred boys needed to be locked up. In the buzz around me I could feel time itself starting to race, I could feel a charge of adrenaline in the air. I wondered if he was feeling it too.

'Well, it won't be long now, I think,' Ramya cut in. 'It looks like the judge is in a hurry to wind up this case.' She paused, a worried look in her eyes. 'I told you already that she is from a conservative Hindu background. But that is not what is bothering me now.'

'What do you mean?'

'I mean: if *I* could feel the heat whenever I went down to Ahmedabad, just imagine the pressures she must be facing. Whatever she decides, she has to live in that state afterwards.' She picked up the papers and put them away in her tote bag. 'We did what we could, Deepi. Now our part in this thing is over.'

27

'Dadi sent these, so I had to bring some for you!' Faiza beamed, holding up a plastic bag full of kesri mangoes. She took one out of the bag and held it up for Adil to see.

It was a lovely golden yellow with a tinge of green. Adil smiled and thought of another promise of rain, which looked at him with eyes almost that colour.

Faiza put the mango back in the bag.

'How is Amma?'

'Better! I told you she had joined work again. From this week she has started to go full time. And these days she is even cooking nice things like she used to.'

'Must be because you are looking chirpy too, Faizoo!'

'No, Bhai. She started making nice food whenever Megha-ben was going to come, and now she does it all the time. She really likes her. They talk about Urdu poetry and things like that.' She paused. 'I should ask Amma to come here and see you now.'

'No,' he shook his head. 'It's not a good idea. I don't want her to see all the police and get upset. Later.'

Faiza nodded. Then she shoved her hand excitedly into the

pocket of her school uniform and brought out a little envelope. 'I almost forgot! I have to give you this too! It has come from Dilnawaz!'

He took the letter from her. It had been opened.

'I didn't open it, Bhai,' she shook her head. 'It was these people in the jail who opened it. To see if it has anything they don't like.'

He nodded. They opened Megha's letters too, but she knew how to say nothing and yet say everything.

'Read it, Bhai.'

He nodded. Dilnawaz's handwriting was neat and careful. Adil had a sudden memory of him sitting at the big wooden table where his father kept his paint supplies and doing his homework solemnly, his feet dangling high above the ground, carefully forming each letter on the page.

'You can read it to me also, Bhai.'

'Okay.

My dear Adil-bhai,

Assalaam aleikum.

How are you? I am fine. I am writing to tell you that we have shifted to Delhi some time back, and we are putting up in a flat near to where we were staying with my Chacha. It is not a full house like we had in Surat, but it is very nice. Nowadays I am in school, but sometimes I go with Baba and my Chacha for painting, if it is a Saturday or Sunday. In our school we also have an Urdu teacher, but I think she is not nice like your mother.

Faiza-ben wrote and told me that they have put you in the jail. It must be some mistake, Adil-bhai, so I am hoping that they will come to know this and let you go again. But you know that even Gandhiji was in the same jail as you in the time of the British, so you must not feel it is only a place for bad

people. I am also praying from my side that they will anyhow take you out
from there fast. Then you have to come to Delhi, and you will stay in our
house. Maybe your mother can also be an Urdu teacher in my school.

Adil-bhai, I remember so much the last day you were there in Surat,
when we helped to make the film. I told you that you and I would make a
film one day. So now I hope that when you come out from the jail and you
shift to Delhi Inshallah that dream of ours will come true.

I am waiting for you.

Your friend,

Dilnawaz

He looked at the letter for a long moment after he had read
it out. Dilnawaz was wise beyond his years. Adil looked up
and saw Faiza watching him closely.

'Yes, Bhai,' she said with quiet finality. 'That is what we
have to do.'

He shook his head. 'You sound very certain.'

'It is the only way, Bhai. You have to be positive. Or you
will lose.'

He put the letter in his pocket and took the mangoes back
to the barrack after his mulaqaat with Faiza. There was a
strange feeling in the air, he thought, as though something
was moving faster, was starting to race, was pulling him and
all the others in its wake. The court hearings were over. The
only thing left now was the judgement.

He sat down and fished in his pocket for the letter, thinking
to read it again. But his fingers found another letter, which
had come from Megha the day before. He pulled it out, and
his eyes went straight to the ending, which was already etched
in his memory.

I am holding my breath and waiting for the day when you and I will
meet again without the grille that keeps us apart.

Hoping with all my heart,

Megha

He felt himself float away on a warm golden cloud. In his daydream, he was on a station platform walking up to her, and she was walking up to him, smiling. He saw her outstretched arms and he walked faster, aching to hold her in his arms again, and this time never let her go . . .

A sudden flash of panic hit him like a whiplash. The dream unravelled.

He sat up abruptly, breathed in deeply and shook his head. Was he mad? How could he even imagine that she would love him the way he loved her? What did she know about him, anyway? He was just a Muslim from Jamalpur tainted forever with the label of terrorist, and rotting away in jail these last three years.

He squeezed his eyes shut, blocking out the moment of anguish. Waiting for it to pass.

He rewound time back to the day he had first met her: the luminous girl in the peach dupatta who had felt strangely guilty about the damage Hindu goons had done. All headscarfed, done up like a Muslim girl, speaking to him in Urdu, enchanted by the long-ago world she imagined to be inside her grandfather's Urdu newspapers. She had told him that she wanted to escape and be anything she wanted to be. Something other than what she was. Other than what her name said she was.

Then the image changed. He was back in her room in the

hostel. The evening light through her window spilling onto their clothes, lying in a heap on the floor. Her voice, soft and husky, whispering his name. Her eyes turning dark and stormy as she began to lose control . . .

He clenched his fists, willed those images away.

Why was she really helping him? Was it love? Had she ever actually told him that she loved him? Or was she again feeling guilty, and trying to make amends for what had been done to him? She liked him. In a way, she now knew him better than ever before, because of the film. She came to Ahmedabad as often as she could. To meet him. But did she *love* him?

'Yes,' he heard. He turned his head in surprise. Had he spoken aloud?

Rasheed was looking at him intently.

'What?' Adil asked.

'I said yes, Adil-bhai. I saw your face looking . . . thoda questionable. So I decide to give you answer.'

'What answer, Rasheed-bhai?'

'Yes. That is the answer. She really, really like you too much.'

Adil smiled bitterly. Rasheed lived in a simpler world. Black and white. If she loved you then, she would love you forever. That was what women did.

'No,' he shook his head, feeling as if a veil had just slipped off his eyes. The real world, he thought. The real world is in shades of blue and grey. Dismal. And forever beyond my reach. 'It is no point thinking about this now. We will never . . .'

'It will happen, Adil-bhai,' Anees's deep voice joined in the conversation. 'The two of you will be together again. This mood of yours is only the darkness below the candle. Not to worry. Everything will be all right. When you leave this place. Only a few more days . . .'

And then Adil felt himself snap.

'Don't talk like that, Anees!' he burst out. 'You *know* they can't let me go!'

'I was only saying . . .'

'Forget it! I told you in the beginning that they wanted to get all the young Muslim men and keep us here forever. So that they would have only frightened females to look at.' He paused, the opening frames of a whole new story playing inside his head. A story he had wished away up to now. 'They want us here so that in time they would be able to forget that there was ever any such thing as Muslim men in Gujarat. Then they could say that Muslims were quiet people who liked pretty things, like poetry, sher-o-shairi, nice people. And keep the men locked up like one more cage of wild animals in the zoo.' His eyes narrowed. '*That* is what they mean when they talk about "diversity".'

'Adil . . .'

'I am tired of putting on a good face! Tired of being good, and not making any trouble. Because in the end it is no use.' He looked away. 'They will always win. And we will lose.' He got up and started to walk away.

'Wait . . .'

'No, Anees-bhai,' he heard Rasheed's voice in Urdu, echoing gently off the barrack walls. 'The boy is right. Leave him alone, let him go and be by himself. You are only making your own self feel good, giving him so much hope.' A pause. 'It is better if he is ready in his mind for whatever verdict the judge is going to give.'

28

'Megha. Do you know what you are doing? How far are you planning to take this thing?'

'What thing, Uncle?'

Her LG let out an exasperated breath. 'You know what I mean. This boy. What is going on?'

'Adil? You know what's going on. We were together, but now he's in jail.'

'Three years is a long time, Megha. I don't know what your feelings for him were then, but . . .'

'It *hasn't* been three years, Uncle. I wish it had! I feel awful that I only got to know he was in jail a few months ago. I should have been one of the first to know!'

'Megha. This is going nowhere. He is *not* going to get out. Understand that! He is in jail as a *terrorist*. It doesn't matter if he did it or not. Are you telling me that you love him so much that you want to put your life on hold for him like this?'

'Maybe.' A pause. 'But how is my life on hold, Uncle? The reason you see me in Ahmedabad so often is my work. I'm supposed to be meeting my guide, but in truth I owe this film to Adil, completely. Nobody else. When I *think* of all the things they did to him to make him confess . . .' She broke off. 'It's *his* life that is on hold,' she added softly.

'What do you really know about him?'

'Uncle!' she exclaimed. 'Would you be talking like this if I told you instead that I was going to have an arranged marriage with a nice boy from a good family in Delhi? Someone I didn't know at all?'

'You mean you are thinking of *marrying* him?'

She laughed. 'Marriage? No! That's a long way off. You don't *start* out in a relationship talking about marriage!'

'In my day . . .'

She shook her head. 'Uncle . . .'

'Listen to me, Megha. I have known you for a long time. And I know what drives you. You feel *responsible* for the whole world, and think it is up to you to set it right. But this is not another test for you to pass, to show how liberal you are. You are crossing a lot of lines here.'

'Do you think I don't know that?' she replied gently. 'I've been told this again and again, by all my friends who saw me with him. I don't know of any other NID girl who ever got involved with a boy from Ahmedabad. Forget Muslim: *any* local boy.'

'Precisely: what do you know about him? Do you know anything at all about his background? His family?'

'I didn't in the beginning. It wasn't important. He was just . . . a warm and caring guy. Different. Interesting. One who didn't go strutting around trying to impress me. Who didn't . . . hit on me. I could actually *talk* to him. Do you ever know more than that when you start a relationship?' A pause. 'But the first time I met him in jail, he asked me to go and meet his mother and his sister. So every time I come, I go and spend time with them. I think now I might even know them better than I know him!' She gave her LG an anguished look. 'Now I even wonder what hurts me more: the thought of him languishing in jail, or what they have to go through, day after day. They are *desperate* to get away from Ahmedabad. But they won't go without him.'

'And what does his mother think? Does she know you are not just a colleague from work? Not just a friend?'

'She figured that out. Very fast.'

'And?'

'You know? I think she was happy. That was the moment she began to come out of her depression. As though she saw that she was not alone any more.'

'I would have thought . . .'

'A few things have changed, Uncle. A lot of women in the Muslim mohallas have had to become stronger, more independent.' She thought a moment. 'And more open-minded.'

'Megha.' He shook his head sadly. 'Maybe I'm not putting this very well. What I mean is that I see you putting so much hope into something that looks impossible. And I see you heading for a lot of heartbreak. Do you really think they are going to let him go?'

'That's not the point, Uncle. I have decided to plan as though he *is* going to get out. Because if he does, that will not be the end of the story. They are going to hound him. They will not leave him alone. And if we are not ready for that, we will lose him again.'

'We?'

'Yes,' she said softly. 'I can't do this without your help.'

'So something *is* going on!' He looked at her thoughtfully for a while. 'And what are you getting me into?'

'Will you help us?'

'Why? Is it something dangerous? Megha, this is not a game. People can be picked up in this town any time on the slightest suspicion . . .'

'No! No. I mean, you don't have to *do* anything!' She stopped, met his look. 'But you're right, Uncle. If they come to know you were involved . . .'

'And it's not just me. I have to think of my family. You want me to expose them too?'

'No . . .' she murmured.

They sat a while in limbo. In silence.

The LG looked around him, at the haven of peace he had managed to preserve. A home where all the turmoil of the last few years had been held at bay. A fantasy world, he thought suddenly. Built on the illusion that 2002 had never happened, and that he lived in a shining and prosperous state. That all was well with the world.

All he needed to do was back off again and take the safe option. Tell this headstrong girl that he couldn't help.

He looked at her again. No, he knew, she would go ahead. With him or without him. And if they picked her up . . .

He stood up at once, shook his head to clear that last thought, and wandered over to the sliding door that opened onto a little patio in the back of the house. He tugged at the cord and lifted the blind. Shielding his eyes against the harsh glare of the summer sun, he turned reluctantly.

'Maybe you had better tell me what you are up to,' he ventured at last.

29

The judge climbed the stairs to her flat and took out the key to the front door. Her nostrils twitched a moment at the aroma coming from inside.

Spices. Meat. Biryani, she decided. Pooja-ben must be cooking up a treat. She opened the door and walked in.

The living room was transformed. There were flowers everywhere, filling all the vases. All the jugs. Little bunches in mugs all over the room. Like a bridal suite.

'Ami-ben!' Pooja-ben exclaimed with a broad smile. 'Ceasefire thay gyu chhe! End of hostilities! So we should celebrate. Tomorrow I'm going back home.' She spun around in a sweeping gesture and pointed to all the flowers. 'This is his peace offering.'

The judge frowned. 'You're going back? I thought you were planning to file for divorce. Think about it, Pooja-ben. This isn't the first time you've wanted to leave him.'

Pooja-ben filled two glasses with ice cubes and poured herself a shot of whisky. The judge's eyebrows went up in amazement.

'And where did you get that? This is supposed to be a dry state.'

'Oh, Ami-ben, you get it everywhere! They deliver it to your home. Pour one for you too?'

To *my* home, the judge thought uneasily. 'I'll just have soda and ice, to keep you company.'

Pooja-ben handed her her soda and flopped down in an easy chair. 'By the way, you have a nice butcher in the neighbourhood.'

'I'll have to take your word for it.'

'Oh no!' Pooja-ben wailed. 'You aren't in one of your veggie moods again?'

The judge shook her head. 'No, if you cooked meat I'll certainly have some. Biryani? That is something I haven't had for a long time!'

'Yes, biryani. Cheers!' She lifted her glass. 'How was your day?'

'Different,' the judge admitted. 'I sat in front of a television screen and watched a videotape. It was submitted in evidence, so I had to see it.'

She thought back to the shaggy looking scribe eagerly writing in the video, and the pale nervous boy in white who was telling his tale, pausing to wait for the scribe to catch up. The biryani now was just the final touch to an unusual day.

Along with Pooja-ben's shock announcement that she would be going back to her husband. The judge looked up at her friend suspiciously. 'So: happily ever after? Like in the fairy tales?'

'I'm not *that* stupid, Ami-ben. I know what he's like. But I know that after this last blowout he is going to be dormant for a good long while. I don't have to look at him. I'll just keep my head down and go about my business.' She slanted a quirky look at her friend. 'And who knows? They say women live longer than men. So I'm probably going to outlive him anyway. Why mess things up at this stage?'

'I see,' the judge said wryly. 'True love.'

'And Neha is coming back for summer holidays next weekend.'

The judge sighed. 'I remember when the two of you had just met. You were the best-looking girl in our class, and he was so much in love with you.'

'He still is, in his way.'

'That was not the impression I got when you came here. When I saw the bruises on your face, I seriously thought of getting you to file charges against him.'

'Like they say: it's complicated. You see . . .' she broke off, finding the right words. 'You see, it isn't as one-sided as it looks. I *do* give it back, and that's what gets him going. If I just sat there meekly, he would either kill me off, or forget about me. But I give just the right amount of resistance.'

'And you call that love.'

'In a way it is.' Pooja-ben gave a lopsided smile. 'You just never thought of it that way.' She put up her hand to stifle the judge's outburst. 'Just think: what does it take to have conflict? Anywhere.' She paused. Cocked her head. 'You need two parties. Right?'

'Not necessarily. You know what I think about . . .'

'Yes, you do!' Pooja-ben cut in swiftly. 'Need two parties. But the beauty of marriage, as opposed to other forms of warfare, is that the result is pre-determined. The man has to win. He's not looking to take chances.'

The judge looked at her friend sceptically.

'But he also wants to be *engaged*,' Pooja-ben continued. 'He wants an adversary he finds *interesting*. Better yet, beautiful. One who does him proud. Someone who looks like she can stand up to him and give it back. He enjoys a good fight.' She shrugged. 'Though she is bound to lose. That is part of the deal.'

'Pooja-ben, this has nothing to do with you giving it back . . .'

'You remember Pakeezah?' Pooja-ben cut in again.

'Pakeezah?'

'Yes.' Pooja-ben waited for the judge to recollect the old, old film. 'Now *she* was every man's dream girl. Lovely. Innocent. Harmless. *Available*. She was a courtesan, right?'

'I'll never understand men. They fantasize about a woman they can never be sure of.'

'What else? It's their old hunting instincts. Now here is Pakeezah. So much grace, such nazaakat, she made all these goons in the audience feel ugly, uncultured. They had to have her, but what they called love included a solid dose of resentment.' Her face clouded, her eyes focused on some distant truth. 'Beware of people who *admire* you. People who say you are *beautiful*. They are not your friends . . .'

Pakeezah . . . The judge gave her friend a long thoughtful look. 'So you're saying that the urge to control and beat up people who are different is . . . the same sort of thing as domestic violence?'

'Well, I didn't exactly say that. But now that you mention it, I'm wondering.'

'You have made me wonder about a few things too, Pooja-ben. And I don't like what I see.'

'Well . . . I've heard of enough cases of things in the home going too far and wives getting killed.' She shrugged. 'But it isn't usually about that, Ami-ben, it isn't usually about hate. It's just a twisted bullying relationship at work. He doesn't *really* want her to go. He just wants her to know her place.'

'As . . .'

'As a *wife*. As a woman. That thing that makes him feel big.'

The judge stared into her glass, watched the little bubbles zing their way to the surface and then fizzle out. Disappear.

'I don't get a good feeling about this decision of yours.'

'Ami-ben,' she said softly, 'I am nothing. I have no career, no home besides the one I just ran away from, no way of keeping myself alive on my own. I wish I had had the sense you had, and gone to college instead of getting married right out of school. But it's too late to change.' She looked out the window into the darkness. 'What I mean is: I do know my place.' She went and poured herself another drink.

The judge waited for her to come back. 'And what is that place?'

'Do you remember when we were in school? We had to do a comprehension passage about a bird that sits in crocodiles' mouths and eats the rotting food stuck in their teeth?'

'The Egyptian plover,' the judge supplied.

'Well, that's more or less what I am, and that's my place now: in the jaws of the crocodile. Most of the time I will be safe there, Ami-ben, because I'm doing something that no one else would do for the crocodile, and he is grateful. He would probably die without me there to look after him. But there will be moments, not too many, but there *will* be moments when he gets carried away and that other side of him will take over, and his jaws will close on me.'

The judge sat in silence and watched her friend finish her drink in one gulp. She *is* a plover bird, she thought. She thinks that she will have to give that up if she is separated from her crocodile. Could it be that the food the plover bird gets from the crocodile's jaws is also an easy addiction, something that takes away its initiative?

An image found its way into her mind, from the courtroom in Sabarmati jail. An image of young under-trials. Some of them had looked like students. They had been certain too, she thought. Certain that the worst was over. They had stayed on, after the riots in 2002, and tried to rebuild their lives in Ahmedabad, not yet ready to cut loose and move on. And they had been right, in that the days of mob violence were over. But that did not mean that their own lives had not been shattered by the same bad feelings, only in a smaller, less apocalyptic form.

She looked at her friend and frowned. 'I think you're very brave to think of going back to him, Pooja-ben. But I am not convinced that your husband has blown off all his steam, or that he will suddenly be transformed into the man you used to know. It looks to me like you are stuck in a rut, and inventing reasons to stay there. You *want* to think you will be safe, because it is the easy way out. But you do know better. Don't you?'

Pooja-ben held her gaze like a trapped deer, said nothing.

'Come,' the judge said. 'Let's have that biryani. After that I need to spend time in my study. I have a judgement to finish.' She stood up. 'And please get rid of all these dead flowers. I think they are going to make me sneeze . . .'

30

It was one of those dreamy early-summer evenings. There was just a hint of a scorch outside, and the humidified air that the desert cooler was bringing down from my terrace had begun to chill my living room. I got up and turned it off, and settled down with just a ceiling fan and a bowl of lychees for comfort, and thought of the two months of summer vacation in store for me after I turned in my grades.

The doorbell. I got up to see who wanted some of my time.

Ramya's tall figure stood in the doorway in a dark-coloured sari, still wearing the legal collar. Cloak and dagger, the words sprang to mind. Clock time vanished. We were back on the POTA trail.

'You aren't busy, are you?' she asked as she breezed in, sat down and slipped off her collar.

'No,' I replied redundantly.

'Okay, let's have a drink.'

I brought a bottle of beer from the fridge and started to pour.

'Uh-uh. You don't have whisky?'

'Help yourself!' I pointed to a small line of bottles, mostly unopened, gifts from friends bringing me one of their two-bottle allowance through Indian Customs. 'Take whatever you like.'

We sat down with our respective drinks.

'So I guess it is Judgement Day.'

'Yes. Cheers!' She took a sip. Put down her drink and picked up her large tote bag. 'And here is the sari you wanted.' She fished inside and brought out a wrapped package.

'You mean . . . we won?'

'Well . . . Not quite,' she admitted. 'You remember that there were eighteen boys in all? Four besides our fourteen?'

I nodded.

'The judge has acquitted thirteen of the boys, which means nine of ours, and also the other four.' A pause. 'The other five got ten-year RI sentences.'

Rigorous Imprisonment. The least one could expect from a POTA conviction.

'What happens next for them?'

'We'll appeal!'

Ten years. I sat and tried to imagine that timespan, sitting in jail. Given the gravity of the charge, making and planting bombs, the judge had awarded surprisingly light sentences.

'The youngest . . . Adil . . . What about him?'

'Acquitted. You always liked him, didn't you?'

'Yes,' I frowned at the qualified success of our efforts. 'That's fantastic news. For him.'

'Well, the confessions were thrown out. You did your job.' She picked up the package. 'So here is the sari.'

'Don't be silly, Ramya!' I shook my head. 'That was just a joke! And in any case, this isn't really a victory.'

She sat back, and the room was silent for a few minutes.

'And the sari isn't silk either,' she sighed. 'You know that, don't you? That I never wear silk?'

I thought of the little silkworms extricated from the forest, put on trays and fed on chopped mulberry leaves, spinning themselves into their cocoons and dreaming of growing up to be moths. Only to find those cocoons forcibly taken away from them when they were done, and soaked to loosen them up and turn them into silk threads. Ending the little creatures' dream of sprouting wings and flying away, back to the mulberry trees and the real jungle.

'No. Some of your saris look shiny so I just assumed. But I guess it makes sense.' My mind zoomed back to our other little friends who had just spent time in captivity, who were also about to sprout wings. 'So thirteen of the boys are now free?'

She paused again. 'Some of them are. But most of them have other cases pending against them. Their acquittal can't come into effect till those cases are cleared too.' She frowned. 'And there is always the possibility of re-arrest. I know of one man who was actually re-arrested the moment he stepped out of the jail.'

'But Adil . . .'

She pulled out a list. 'Your Adil is free. For the moment.'

'For the moment?'

'Yes. He had better get the hell out of Gujarat while the going is good. I can just see the cops eyeing him as he tries to go about his daily life. They probably think they own him now!'

31

Acquitted!

The echo of the judge's words rang inside his head, the sound multiplying and renewing itself until it sparkled. He was free! Up until now he had not let himself think about the possibility. Nazar na lagey, he had thought. Avert your eyes. To look is to invite bad luck.

The bright noise died down. Silence. He was still in Sabarmati jail, in the courtroom, standing behind the wooden railing at the back with the others.

Anees . . . His heart clenched.

He felt his friend's arm reach around his shoulders and give him a warm hug. He looked up, forced himself to meet his eyes. Heard his deep voice, he was saying something . . .

'. . . to feel happy, Adil-bhai,' his words suddenly became audible. 'You knew I was not going to get off so easily. I told you it would take a miracle. But you . . .' he smiled, shrugging off his own bad news, 'you are free, brother! Half of my dream has come true. Mubarak!'

They stayed together as they were led back to the jail, knowing that they would have to be separated when the jail authorities got their copy of the judgement. The one thing he had never imagined was that he would be wishing for time to slow down at this point, for these last few moments to go on and on.

Then Anees and the four others who had been convicted were taken aside.

Adil went back with the others to his old under-trial barrack. He had fifteen minutes to collect his belongings and say his goodbyes.

Rasheed was waiting for him. He raised his hand to his forehead in a sort of military salute as he saw Adil. His face showed no surprise.

'I will miss you, Rasheed-bhai.'

'You are leaving the jail at right time, Adil-bhai. Before mosquitoes come. Please give my salaams to your mother and sister.' He paused. 'And to your friend, the lady cloud. Khuda hafiz.'

And soon it was time to go. He was led away to the front entrance. The first barred gate opened, and then the last. He went under the archway and through the door of a doorless house like the sky.

Faiza was standing on the road waiting, talking urgently into a cell phone. She saw him, cut the call and came running, hugged him with all her might.

'Bhaiiii!!! At last!'

A young man got down from the driver's seat of a waiting rick. 'Salaam w'aleikum, Adil-bhai,' he said shyly. 'It is good to have you back.'

Zafar-bhai. His neighbour. Faiza had made him her

accomplice on the mission to receive him. Adil wrapped his arms around him.

'Come, Bhai,' he heard her say urgently. 'Let us get out of here.'

They had barely started on their way when the cell phone rang again.

'He's here,' he heard Faiza say. She handed him the phone. 'Hello?'

'Adil!'

'Megh . . .' he breathed, not trusting his voice to say more.

'My Adil! This is the *best* happy ending! Faiza just told me! I can't wait to see you!' A glowing pause. 'But don't relax yet. It isn't over. You're ready for Plan A?'

An image of their first mulaqaat flashed before his eyes. And his promise to Faiza. 'Yes. What do I have to do?'

'Okay, listen. You go with Faiza now. She's taking you to my LG's home. Your Mom is waiting for you there. You are not to go back to Jamalpur.' A pause. 'Faiza has packed all your things. When you get to my LG's, go and bathe, shave off your beard, and get out of those jail clothes. And stay out of sight.'

'Okay.'

'Tomorrow you wear your new clothes and take a bus to Jaipur. Don't come by train. You mustn't book any ticket that will leave a computer trail. You are going to disappear. Can you do that?'

'Yes.'

'Then I'll come and receive you there. Tomorrow.'

He handed the phone back to Faiza after she rang off.

'No, Bhai,' she shook her head. 'It's yours. We got it for you in Zafar-bhai's name, so it is safe: they don't have this number. You will need it, to stay in touch with her.'

He slipped the phone into his pocket. Looked out the sides of the rick, trying to get his bearings.

'This place has changed a bit. And in any case, I told him to take a different route, and mix with other autos, so that they can't make out which one is us and try to follow.'

A few more turns and they were out of the traffic and headed for a familiar neighbourhood. He thought of the time Megha had phoned him, that night, and how he had escorted her to her LG's home. The place still exuded a sense of peace.

They stopped in front of a bungalow hidden by trees and a lot of greenery.

'Come,' Faiza said imperiously.

He followed her through the little garden gate. The front door was open, and he stepped out of the sunlight and immediately found himself in a large cool room. His mother rose to meet him.

She looked older. Three whole years had passed since he had seen her! But her face lit up at once. He put his arms around her and she sobbed in relief.

'Amma!' Faiza's voice rang out from behind him. 'Let him go and change his clothes! And Bhai, you must not take those clothes with you tomorrow. Here,' she handed him a rugged-looking backpack. 'Your new clothes are in this. These jeans should fit.'

He stood under the shower and let the water run over him, torrents of water, rinsing away three years of his life. It was this shower — the seemingly endless supply of water, the sudden *privacy* — that convinced him that he was not dreaming, that his time in jail had really come to an end. He stepped out of the shower and picked up a thick soft towel and dried himself, and stared at his face in the mirror.

He had grown older too. The face he knew had been a boy's face. He saw a pair of scissors Faiza must have left for him and used them to snip off his beard. Collected the hair carefully and threw it into the little bin. Then he lathered his face and shaved.

He pulled out a pair of jeans from the backpack and chose a T-shirt to wear with it, turned to see himself in the mirror. A young college student looked back, smiling as he smiled. He bent and gently rolled up his old izaar-kurta and left them with all their memories in a corner of the bathroom.

Then he went out barefoot into the living room, enjoying the feel of the cool red cement floor on the soles of his feet. His mother saw him and poured his chai.

He sat in the comfortable chair and felt himself being enveloped in a warm silken cocoon, let the sound of Faiza's chatter splash over him, and his mother's gentler voice interjecting from time to time. He felt he could sit there forever, just listening to them talk about this and about that.

In his mind's eye an image appeared, an image of a moth, still a pupa, lying encased in a cocoon and dreaming dreams of flight. He had once seen a picture of a moth with atrophied wings: a moth that had been helped to emerge from its cocoon. It was supposed to have come out on its own steam, used its baby wings to beat its way out of its shell, because only that effort would strengthen its muscles and make its wings large and capable of flight when it was finally free.

Megh had said she thought of him as a moth, drawn to the light. Had she been thinking of this particular moth when she had decided to make him come alone by bus to Jaipur?

He excused himself and went out into the tiny backyard and called her.

She picked up the phone at once.

'Hi,' he said. 'You are amazing. How did you get the idea of making me come part-way by bus? It's just what I need, to learn to find my way again.'

'I wanted to come,' she cut in. 'But my LG told me to stay in Delhi. And I thought, well, until it was certain . . .'

Nazar, he thought. 'I know. I didn't allow myself to even *think* about it before it actually happened.'

'And I didn't want to draw attention to you. Easier if one anonymous man takes a bus ride, na?'

'I'll manage,' he said. 'Don't worry. But when we meet, you might not be able to recognize me! I don't think I recognize myself now.'

She laughed. 'I'll recognize your clothes! And my own backpack. Faiza decided that you should look like an IIT student. So we went and got your clothes together.' She shifted gears, her voice soft and guarded. 'It's going to be a tense time for you tomorrow, Adil. Now it's your show. You'll have to control your impulses, slow down and play by the script. Don't let yourself get spooked. Remember: you are just another student going somewhere for his summer holidays.'

Megha's LG showed him to his room after dinner that night, and turned on the cooler and the overhead fan. He gave Adil a fresh towel and indicated the attached bathroom.

'I hope you will be comfortable,' he said anxiously.

Adil's mind reeled at the irony. Comfortable! The script, he remembered. 'Yes, thank you,' he said simply. 'Everything is great.'

'Good night, then. See you in the morning.'

And then there was just the hum of the cooler and the ceiling fan for company. He was alone again.

He woke up once during the night, felt the soft pillow under his head and was transported back to another night, a lifetime ago, when he had woken up in the dark in a strange place. Vijay's home. And heard the voice of a large man who was certain that he would not be harmed. But the man had died, and that same day Adil had become a marked man.

Vijay, he thought. I will not see him before I go . . .

He drifted back to sleep and dreamt of Vijay on patrol in the Dangs forest with a bow and arrow, and his hair in a topknot.

He woke up just before six, looked around and remembered where he was. He washed up and wore his jeans and a fresh T-shirt and went down the stairs.

The living room was deserted, but he could hear the LG's old mother in a little room near the kitchen pottering around, getting ready for her morning puja. She saw Adil and called him over.

'Taari yatra mate shubhkamna.'

He went and sat with her, curious but uneasy. For his safe journey?

'Chinta na kar,' she smiled reassuringly.

'She knows, Bhai.' Faiza's voice broke in softly in English. He turned and saw her take her place next to him. 'She knows you won't pray to the idols. She just wants you to sit there while she does her puja.'

The old woman picked up a little bell and closed her eyes. She rang the bell like a metronome, marking time as she silently recited a shloka. She put down the bell and lit a single diya with a long handle, and ended her puja with an aarti to the framed images of Lakshmi and Narayan. Then she turned to Adil with a warm smile and reached for his right hand.

'She wants to tie a puja thread on you, Bhai.'

He gave her his hand, felt a tingle as she wound the red thread around his wrist and gently put a tika, a touch of red powder, on his forehead.

'Aayushmaan bhava,' she said formally in Sanskrit. May you have a long life.

'This will keep you safe, Bhai. Now you are no more Adil: you are Aditya!'

His eyes widened as he looked down at his alien wrist. He opened his mouth to thank the old woman . . .

'But don't make the mistake of trying to speak in Gujarati,' Faiza went on. 'You sound like a mullah now! They will find some crime they need a suspect for and take you straight back to jail.' She looked him firmly in the eye. 'Stick to English. Anybody asks you anything, you answer in English. Best if they don't even understand you.'

At breakfast Megha's LG asked him about the plan of action.

'Megha wants me to take a bus to Jaipur. Today. She says she will come and meet me there.'

The older man nodded. 'You will have to go to Paldi bus depot, then. That is where you will get an interstate bus. I think they mostly leave in the evening, and do the journey overnight. So now you have the day to . . . chill.' He smiled. 'I'll check the bus timings for you.' He pointed to the newspapers lying on a chair in the living room. 'And you might as well catch up with what's going on in the world.'

Adil saw his mother sigh, saw the light in her eyes fade. 'So little time!' she murmured. 'I get you back after all these years only to lose you again the next day . . .'

Faiza sprang to attention. 'No, Amma! Don't worry! We are going to Delhi too, very soon. As soon as he calls to say he is there. But *we* will not have to do all this tamasha, hiding and going. When it is our turn to go, you and I are going to *fly*!' she exulted. 'Then it won't even matter if they know we are going. In fact, I don't think they will even be looking for us.'

The day went by like a series of vignettes. Adil filed them away in his mind as memories. All too soon it was evening, and time to go.

His mother handed him a wallet with money for the journey.

'And I made sure you have change, Bhai,' Faiza put in. 'You don't want to look like a spy, only carrying big bills.' She dug into his backpack and pulled out a pair of dark-rimmed glasses and put them on him. 'Here!' she exclaimed. 'You need some more disguise! These make you look *soooo* studious. Like you really need a break for the holidays. Go and see yourself in the mirror, Bhai!'

The LG's driver dropped him off outside the terminal. It was already dark. He got out of the car, shouldered the backpack, paused briefly on the pavement where he and Megha had walked holding hands, then headed inside and found his bus. There was still a half-an-hour till departure. He put his backpack down and waited on the platform, his ears naturally picking up the sounds around him, Gujarati accents he had not heard in the last three years. Faiza was right: he did sound like a mullah.

In the distance he saw a group of policemen.

It was too late in the day for hafta, he thought, the weekly bribe money they would come in a large group and take from the vendors. Protection money. So what were they all doing here now?

And then his heart lurched. He suddenly felt faint.

They were looking for him.

Only yesterday the five of them had been released from jail. And up to now no POTA detenu had ever gone free in Gujarat. It stood to reason that he would now be trying to leave Ahmedabad.

They had come to re-arrest him.

The police headed his way.

As he looked down to check on his backpack, his eyes caught the puja thread around his wrist. He was now Aditya, he remembered. He was safe.

He looked up a moment at the overhead signs, avoiding their eyes. Then he calmed himself, forced himself to level his gaze and look at them, through them, focusing on a point in the distance.

One of them was looking straight at him.

'Kya jaas, dikra?'

The script, Adil remembered. Follow the script. I am just another student going for summer holidays.

And do not talk like a mullah. Speak English.

'Bombay . . .' he said.

Silence. The cop turned abruptly and said something to the others.

Why did I say Bombay?

That's the *first* place someone running away would think to go!

He brought his right hand up and tried to steady his nerves by tucking away the end of his puja thread.

A younger policeman noted his puja thread and nodded, stepped forward. 'This is not the right place,' he said. 'You have to go over there.' He pointed further along the platform. '*That* bus is going to Mumbai.'

Adil let out his breath as softly as he could. 'Thanks.' He shouldered his backpack and ambled off.

Out of the corner of his eye he watched them, saw them head out of the depot. He came back slowly to his earlier spot. The bus to Jaipur was beginning to load up.

Ten minutes to go.

I'll call Megh as soon as we leave, he decided.

He took a last glance around and said his goodbyes to Ahmedabad.

32

I sat alone in the departure lounge in pre-dawn light rewinding to my last flight to Ahmedabad five years ago.

In a sense, Ramya was sending me on this trip too. Just a few weeks earlier, we had sat together at a garden party on a balmy evening and talked about those days. And under the fairy lights in the trees, she had suggested that I might want to meet some of the boys who had been released.

The idea grew in my mind, and I decided to take her up on it. A few weeks later I phoned her and asked her how to get in touch with them.

'You can't,' she replied tersely. 'They're in jail.'

'But . . .'

'They have other cases pending against them.'

'But weren't some of them freed?'

A pause. 'Then they must have been re-arrested. As far as I know no POTA prisoner in Gujarat has been freed.' Another pause. 'Can we talk later? I'm busy in court.'

So I called her again that evening.

'Deepi, I *did* try to find out for you. But people there said that the boys are still in jail.'

'Don't you at least have the paperwork? A copy of the judgement? I thought you brought it all back to Delhi!'

'It's all in Ahmedabad. In a box somewhere in the office. Or with the lawyer who is handling the appeal. Deepi . . .'

'Yes?'

'The whole thing is so . . . muddy. Everyone I asked said they are still in jail, but the reasons they gave me are all different. And it doesn't add up. So I don't know what to think.'

'What about Apoorva-bhai?'

'He must be out of India. I tried to get him. He isn't picking up.'

My mood sank below sea level. Had it all been for nothing?

Summer holidays were coming up. And I had never used my Leave Travel Allowance, which would cover the cost of one trip within India per year. I decided to make a trip to Ahmedabad and see for myself.

Ramya eventually sent me an email, copying me into a mail to Apoorva-bhai, asking him to help me. He was out of town at the moment, she told me. But he was expected back around the time I got to Ahmedabad. He might know something.

My flight was called. I boarded and found my seat. It was more cramped than I remembered.

The stewardess came around after take off with a high-wattage smile, offering me snacks for sale.

We made our descent into Ahmedabad through a bank of grey clouds. Monsoon was about to hit. It came a month earlier here, I remembered. In Delhi it was still the dry heat of summer. I picked up my backpack and went down the steps, ready for that familiar short walk.

Brand new buses stood there on the tarmac, waiting to take deplaning passengers to the terminal.

I entered the new terminal building, ready to walk straight through as I always did, since I had no checked baggage. But the exit was to the side now, and it led into an arrival hall as slick and modern as one in a Delhi airport.

Jaafer-bhai had come to pick me up in his brand-new cherry-red Santro. He directed an AC vent towards me as we waited in line to pay and leave the parking lot.

The billboards along the route from the airport were now mostly in English. I tried to orient myself, looking out for the little underpass on the way where the road was supposed to dip and curve. Where was it?

Jaafer-bhai smiled proudly. 'Now, Madam, Ahmedabad becoming *almost* parallel to metro city.'

But the entrance to the hotel was the same, though in daylight it lacked the gloomy look that had stuck in my mind from my first visit. I checked in and was shown to a room without the dark wood panelling and dull wallpaper I remembered. It looked large and full of light.

Jaafer-bhai and I nosed around awhile in the lobby, looking for the conference room where we had done the mock interviews, working out where we each had sat, and where the camera would have been. We walked down the stairs to the basement and found the restaurant where we had had our dinner early in the morning, before my first deposition in Sabarmati jail. And we tried to find the suite where we had worked the first night.

'Now I take you to see Shah Alam dargah,' Jaafer-bhai

announced grandly. 'Which was refugee camp during riots. It is on the *outer* skirts of Ahmedabad.'

'Then I'd better change my clothes,' I mused. 'And I should take a dupatta.'

We headed south, past the new BRT corridor. The people on the roadsides took on an increasingly Islamic look, the men with skullcaps and beards and short white pajamas. Jaafer-bhai parked near the main entrance and I slipped my dupatta over my head.

We entered the premises under a tall arch and I tried to get my bearings. Shama had been here, and she had said something about the place having an L-shape. The only L-shaped area seemed to be a graveyard, running all along the southern wall to the right, and continuing behind the main building.

'Refugees were putting up on graves only,' Jaafer-bhai explained. 'Now I show you a *famous* tree. More than 500 years old.' He looked around uncertainly. 'Onto this tree ladies used to tie mannats, Madam, means: prayers. And this would give milk. For babies.'

'What sort of tree?' I asked, trying to be helpful.

'Is banyan tree, Madam. Should be here only, with chabutra . . .'

A withered dried tree stood there in the chabutra in front of us, a bone-white skeleton stretching its long skinny arms up at the uncaring sky. We asked the mullahs if this was the tree.

Yes, they replied. It was a very old tree. It had been there for at least 500 years, from the time the dargah was built. Shah Alam himself had known it and loved it. Just a few years ago it had dried up. But they hadn't had the heart to cut it down.

On the drive back into town, Jaafer-bhai was pensive. 'I think maybe tree died after seeing so much suffering,' he said at last. 'Too many people, and no other place to find milk.'

We sat down for lunch in a vegetarian restaurant, not too far from the place I planned to pick up spices, pickles and khakra to take back to Delhi. I told Jaafer-bhai the real reason for my visit.

'I remember that day,' he mused. 'Is true, what you are saying. I think five boys managed to leave the jail. Names were given in newspaper.' He shook his head. 'But I did not keep copy.'

'Were they re-arrested?'

'I did not hear about such a thing.' He shook his head again, dispelling the idea. 'I myself have gone to the jail for mulaqaat, and people in my family are going, all the time. My cousin-brother is there, was under-trial at that time. In same barrack as boys. If this thing had happened, would have been *big* news inside the jail.'

All of a sudden I felt light enough to fly!

'Is there any news about them?' I pressed him further. 'I mean: what they are doing now?'

He shook his head again. 'No. No news . . .'

I had fixed an appointment that evening to meet another lawyer who worked with the Muslim community. Jaafer-bhai came with me, and we sat in the waiting room with some Muslim-looking men and a calm, friendly-seeming woman in a black burqa who sounded like a schoolteacher.

On one side of the room, a number of scribes sat at old desktop computers, taking down verbatim testimony in Gujarati. We got up to watch.

'Sixty words per minute!' I calculated. 'Right?'

One of the scribes nodded. 'I can also do sixty words per minute in shorthand.'

'Me too!' Jaafer-bhai chimed in.

'But not in longhand,' I suggested.

'No,' the scribe agreed. 'Nobody can do that fast. In fact . . .' his eyes got a faraway look as he chased a distant memory, 'in fact, there was case a few years back. It was about that only. About whether sixty words per minute was possible in longhand. They had brought handwriting expert from Delhi.'

Jaafer-bhai grinned broadly. At least among scribes we were famous.

An elderly client came out of the lawyer's office and I was shown in. I spent the first few minutes dropping every name I knew in the human rights pantheon while the lawyer eyed me suspiciously. At last he unfroze, and sent for chai for both of us.

But he had no good news to give. As far as he knew, there had been no POTA prisoners released. He was certain of it.

Tomorrow, I thought. I'm meeting Apoorva-bhai tomorrow morning. So far the news is fifty-fifty. And Jaafer-bhai is closer to the ground.

I got back to the hotel after dark. I decided to stay in my room, not to call anyone I knew in town and try to fix an evening. Tomorrow, I thought. I fell asleep with my fingers crossed.

It rained in the early hours of the morning. A light pre-monsoon shower. When I went out to catch a rick to Apoorva-bhai's flat the air was crisp and cool, and the trees newly washed.

I sat in Apoorva-bhai's study and waited for him to come with our chai. One of his desktop computers had blue-screened and would need re-formatting, I thought. I hoped the other one was working.

We sat down and sipped a few moments, and then I told him about last night's meeting, where the lawyer had been certain that the boys were still all in jail.

'I've heard that story too,' he smiled. 'But these people don't really know. Some of the boys who were acquitted *are* still in jail: that is true. But that is not to say that *all* of the boys have been held back. The police have no discretion in this.' He handed me a printout, a list of names, fathers' names and addresses with five entries highlighted in yellow: the boys who had had no other cases pending.

'Are you saying that these five boys are free?' I asked incredulously.

'As far as I know,' he shrugged.

'What does that mean?'

He paused to weigh his words carefully. 'It means that there is no record of them having being arrested for anything else. They are not in judicial custody in the state of Gujarat.'

'But they could have been taken into police custody?'

'They could have been, but unless they were killed — and we have no record of any encounter deaths involving them — then where would they be now, if not in jail? And they are not there.'

'So could I meet them? Where do you think they are?'

'I am not in touch with them,' he shrugged. 'I am not from the community, so I don't have any inside information about them. They *might* still be in Ahmedabad, for all you know. But my best guess is that they would have left town.' He paused. 'I think I even advised them to go.'

Was it as easy as that? No record of them in jail, or dead in encounters, and I could just assume that they were free?

'I'm not convinced,' I went on doggedly. 'I mean, just because you don't have bodies to show doesn't mean the police didn't get them and do away with them. After all . . .'

Apoorva-bhai's eyes grew pensive at once. 'I'm not saying it is impossible, what you're talking about. It happens all the time in Kashmir. Young boys abducted by the military and then disappearing. And then some of them are eventually traced to mass graves in remote areas.' He paused, tried to make up his mind. 'But there are a few differences here: there is no army involvement in Gujarat . . .'

'But the Gujarat police . . .'

'Yes, I know.' He cut in. 'I know the police here are not angels. But I think it is unlikely that these boys got picked up and then vanished into thin air.'

'You're just guessing.'

'No. What was the basis of Ramya's claim that they are back in jail? Do you know? Because if that is what you're going on, I can tell you that they aren't.'

'I have no idea,' I conceded.

'Ramya never had any interactions with the boys, you know. She wanted to stay away from any personal involvement in the case. They were hounding her, and looking for anything at all they could get to discredit her. So she always left that part of the work to me.' He rested his case. 'That is all I can say. You have to make up your own mind.'

So I was left with just a strong probability: that five of the boys must have sprouted wings and flown. To places safer than the best witness protection programmes could have devised for them. Like the children one loses to adulthood, they had vanished out of our lives. I had to take that as the final word, and as my only glimpse of success.

As I walked down the street, the air around me was bright and full of birdsong. I opened up my sights to a wide-angle view of the city and got out my phone to find my old friends.

The first friend I tried did not pick up my call, though his phone kept ringing. He had also not taken my call when I had tried his number a few times from Delhi. I sent him a cryptic text message: no nouns, only pronouns, nothing that could remotely be said to incriminate him.

Another friend, a cartoon animator, picked up my call instantly.

'Hi. I'm in Ahmedabad, and . . .'

'Let's meet for lunch,' he cut in swiftly. 'We can talk then.'

I had never known him to be anything but open and innocent. And completely clueless about politics.

We had our lunch in a little restaurant near Law Garden and talked about cartoons. And as we talked, a story faded up inside my head, a story I had read many years ago. Of a group of wild rabbits making a journey, and stopping at a rabbit farm full of large healthy-looking animals, all obsessively satisfied with their lot. Every so often one of the farm rabbits would be caught in a wire trap and harvested as food, and would vanish, while the others looked resolutely away, redoubling their faith in the system that was keeping them larger and better fed than their friends in the wild. Until one day, when the largest rabbit himself was trapped, and had to acknowledge the existence of the wires in order to free himself.

I got back to my hotel room early that evening, while it was still daylight. I opened the curtains and looked out at the Sabarmati river.

The Sabarmati that I remembered had been just a tiny trickle in the summer flowing at the centre of a wider flood plain. Now the banks were being reinforced, their height raised, in anticipation of a constant supply of water, diverted from the dammed up Narmada river.

Kshirasagar. The word came to mind suddenly. The cosmic ocean of milk. The source of the milk had shifted from a 500-year-old tree, beloved of Shah Alam, to a controversial man-made dam that had submerged virgin forest and created homeless tribal refugees. Why did 'development' always involve so much human sacrifice? Between the old town and the new town a river of milk would flow, set in motion by a man who would be king. Or, some said, God.

I turned away from the window, focused my attention on the list I had brought back from Apoorva-bhai's study. With young Adil's name highlighted prominently at the top. At that moment, the Sabarmati river and all its new-found milk faded into insignificance. Outside the window, the sun had begun its final descent. The day was done.

Adil, I thought. Where are you now? Which one of the young men I pass on the street in some other city of India will actually be you? Will I ever know?

I fell asleep on this note of uncertainty.

The next morning, the grey clouds were back to playing aankh-michauli. I went down to the back lawn, near the river, and felt a few raindrops, just for a moment. Then the light faded up and the clouds retreated.

Jaafer-bhai came to take me to the airport. My flight was not until noon, but I was already packed. As we lingered over chai, I remembered the one thing I had promised myself I would take back to Delhi. Kesri mangoes.

We made a detour back to Lal Darwaza, and Jaafer-bhai and I chose a dozen kesri mangoes, some big, some small.

'This is promise of rain,' he said with satisfaction, cradling one in his hand.

The golden fruit looked back at me like it had a secret to share.

Inside the terminal, I stopped and packed the mangoes into my backpack along with the khakra, the spices and the pickles. The backpack would now go as checked-in luggage.

I sat and waited in the new unfamiliar departure lounge and watched the rain clouds return. Our flight was called, we boarded the gleaming buses. As I climbed the steps to the plane, the first cool breeze began to blow.

I found my seat and buckled up, no longer feeling cramped. We taxied off to join the queue waiting at the runway.

And then we were off. For a long moment we were up alongside the monsoon clouds, listening in on their turbulent conversation.

And then the wheels folded below us and we took flight, leaving Ahmedabad and the POTA trail far behind.

Acknowledgements

This story would never have occurred to me, or grown into a book, were it not for:

Nitya Ramakrishnan, who brought me into her legal work twice, and taught me most of what I know about the Indian legal system.

Somnath Vatsa, who was there in person and on email to clear doubts about legal issues as I wrote.

Zakia Soman, who shared the precious interviews she had done with young men in Sabarmati jail, and was on hand to answer all my questions.

Shivani Mohan and Imrana Qadeer, who told me in vivid detail all that they had seen during the violence in Ahmedabad in 2002 and in the relief camps.

Fr. Cedric Prakash SJ, Sanjiv and Shweta Bhatt and D.P. Bhattacharya, who gave me information and connected me to people I needed to meet.

Anindo Banerji, who told me whatever I needed to know about Sabarmati jail.

Dinesh Mohan and Dunu Roy, who shared with me all their findings about the Godhra train fire.

Jug Suraiya, for the story about ghosts leaving the graveyard on a day of fire.

Anil Patel and Rohit Bhan, for checking out details about the geography of Ahmedabad and Gujarat as I wrote.

Shruti Narayan, Akhil Paul, Hakim Raja and Nitin Desai, for help with the Gujarati dialogue.

Mathew Varghese, for all the medical details.

Shivani Mohan, Mathew Varghese, Imrana Qadeer and Meghana Acharya, for reading the manuscript and helping me to bring the characters to life.

Manu Joseph, who gave me the first bits of information I needed to get started.

Ajitha G.S. of HarperCollins India, for her enthusiasm and constant presence on email.

My publisher, V.K. Karthika, whose idea it was that I should drop everything else and just write this story I kept telling her, and making sure I missed nothing.

All the others who helped, in Ahmedabad and via email, but who did not want to be mentioned.